AMMA DARKO lives
University of Science a
spent in Germany she returned to Ghana in 1987.

Darko is the author of the novel which was originally published in Germany as *Der Verkaufte Traum* (Schmetterling Verlag, 1991) and published in the original English as *Beyond the Horizon* (Heinemann, 1995). She is a Fellow of the Cambridge Seminar. She is married and has three children.

AMMA DARKO

THE HOUSEMAID

Heinemann

Heinemann is an imprint of Pearson Education limited, a company incorporated in England and Wales, having its registered office at Edinburgh Gate, Harlow, Essex, CM20 2JE.
Registered company number: 872828

www.heinemann.co.uk

Heinemann is a registered trademark of Pearson Education Limited

First published in 1998

British Library Cataloguing in Publication Data
A catalogue record for this book is available from the British Library

Cover design by Touchpaper
Cover illustration by Alan Bond

Phototypeset by SetSystems Ltd, Saffron Walden, Essex

Printed by Multivista Global Ltd

ISBN: 978 0 435910 08 2

20 19 18 17 16 15 14
IMP 20 19 18 17 16 15 14 13 12 11

Part 1

Chapter 1

In Ghana, if you come into the world a she, acquire the habit of praying. And master it. Because you will need it, desperately, as old age pursues you, and mother nature's hand approaches you with a wry smile, paint and brush at the ready, to daub you with wrinkles.

If, on top of this, your children, waging a desperate war of their own for economic survival, find themselves having too little time for you, count you among the forsaken and forgotten; and if, crowning it all, cash, fine sweet cash, decides it doesn't really fancy your looks and eludes you in all nooks, crooks and crannies, then know for sure that you are on route to qualifying grandly as a witch.

A dejected widow, once upon a time a vibrant akpeteshie seller in the village of Braha, now penniless, aged and lonesome, started towards 'witchdom' when one of her grandchildren developed kwashiorkor. She had turned herself into a snake and lodged inside the poor child's stomach, they said.

Then another grandchild got a goitre. And all eyes in Braha saw red.

'What is she doing lodging in parts of her grandchildren's bodies like that?' they asked. And formally pronounced her a witch.

They drove her to live in an isolated hut on the outskirts of the village. No one helped her except a few sympathisers who dropped off leftovers as they passed on their way to their farms.

Near the hut were several paths, but beyond that there was only bush. Which was why the old woman grew suspicious when she noticed a thick trail of black ants travelling to and from the thicket behind her hut. She made her suspicions known, but got what any witch talking serious talk should get: jeers.

'Why not check your sorcery pot,' she was advised. 'Could be a couple of your toads met their untimely deaths while trying to defect.' To roars of laughter.

But the old widow persisted, insisting on a search of the thicket. And when she saw that no one responded, she defied her isolation and showed up on the steps of the village elder's home. His household was thrown into turmoil. What else but ill luck could result from a witch showing up at dawn on your doorstep? Best satisfy her and be rid of her. So a search was ordered.

The young men, whose task this was, were incensed.

'If we find nothing, we will drive her even farther into the bush,' they threatened.

But no sooner were they at the edge of the thicket than they were confronted by a foul and pungent odour. The search gathered fervour. Then they stumbled upon it – the gruesome, decaying corpse of a newborn baby girl.

Braha was in uproar.

Who did this? Whose child was it? What a hideous and unforgivable deed! And why did the gods allow it to happen?

'Do you think it was already dead when it was abandoned?' someone wondered.

'I hope so. I hate to consider the possibility of it having been left there still breathing,' replied another.

'God helps us!'

'Yes. After which the gods should also fish out the culprit. Division of labour!'

◆

Braha was too small a community to have a police station of its own, so the police in the next big village, Osiadan, were notified. And they in turn made a report to the regional police, who quickly dispatched two officers to Braha.

By the following morning, both national and local papers had got wind of the story, and made headlines of it.

'WERE THE GODS ASLEEP?' asked one local headline. And another: 'FIND THE MOTHER! HANG HER!'

But the two national papers were less sensationalist. 'WHY DID SHE DO IT?' asked the first. And the second: 'MOTHERHOOD ON TRIAL!'

A fervent search for the mother began, and anyone with any information at all was urged to call at the nearest police station.

◆

In the midst of the uproar, two boy scavengers searching the rubbish dump as usual for anything that might be useful, spotted a red plastic bag and made a grab for it. Inside they found a faded pink, white and yellow flowered blouse, some beige nylon underwear and a faded cover cloth. All of these were stained with plenty of blood and other fluids the two scavengers could make no sense of. But they took it all anyway, because they had come across finds in worse states which had turned out good and useful.

Back home they gave their discovery to their ten-year-old babysitter, the sister of one of them. She soaked the clothes in a bucket of water and waited for her mother to come home from market so that she could get 200 cedis for a bar of soap to wash them.

◆

By now the abandoned baby's story had spread to every nook and corner, causing fights and arguments in many camps. Suddenly the name of an unknown eastern village was on the lips of every Ghanaian.

At the station near the main market in Kumasi, the town where the two scavengers made their find, a male truck pusher, scarred by a tribal mark on his left cheek, was loading a woman's yams. He shouted across to no one in particular, 'As for this, when the mother is caught, her womb should be removed, cut in two, and given to her to swallow by the count of three.'

'Yes!' agreed a second truck pusher, eager for blood, as he haggled with a tomato seller. Baring his badly stained teeth, he yelled, 'And she shouldn't be anaesthetised when the womb is being removed.'

'Rubbish!' butted in the tomato seller, who could take no more of this male nonsense. 'I can see you two young men turning out just like the irresponsible man who impregnated the poor woman in the first place.'

'Madam! Ah!' The scarred truck pusher was at a genuine loss. 'Who said he was irresponsible? And as for him, what does he even have to do with the abandonment of the baby?'

This so infuriated the woman with the yams that she spat angrily right at the scarred truck pusher's feet. He seethed with disgust.

The yam woman didn't give a hoot.

'You holy fool!' she roared. 'You think the mother just sat

there, opened her legs, and God above pushed the baby into her or what?'

'Oh!' cried stained teeth, unable to hold his tongue, 'Oh! Why? Did my brother say it wasn't a man who impregnated her? Is that the issue?'

'Good question, my brother. Ask that again.' A taxi driver parked nearby and busily feasting on boiled corn and salted coconut, interrupted. 'Why do women always try to turn issues around like that? The issue is why she should deliver a baby and dump her in the thicket, not . . .'

'Shut up! SHUT UP!' the tomato woman shouted. 'Why do you men always try to make nonsense of issues, just to escape blame?'

'Escape blame? Please madam!' the truck pusher with the stained teeth sneered. 'Tell me,' to the taxi driver, 'can you understand why whenever trouble to do with sex crops up, women talk as if it was only men who enjoyed the act?'

The taxi driver applauded wildly. 'How you have hit the nail right on the head, my brother!' To more cheers, which disgusted the tomato seller.

'This is getting nowhere,' she blurted out. And turned her frustration on her truck pusher. 'You either take what I am offering, or me and you have no deal.'

'Why?' stained teeth shrieked. 'Ah! Are you mad at me because of what I said?'

'Why should I be?' with caustic sarcasm. 'The poor baby's mother, whoever she is, is no relation of mine, so why should I be mad with you over her? All that I'm interested in is paying you the lowest possible price to cart my tomatoes. That's all.'

The all-male cart pushers realised that they had better not provoke their all-female customers any further.

'Then as for this, my brother, let me shut my big mouth up,

before my madam customer here decides to let someone else cart her yams,' quipped the scarred pusher.

And all, including the taxi driver, laughed.

◆

But it wasn't a laughing matter everywhere. At a nearby taxi station close to the market, it turned into a real fight when two drivers disagreed on who was guilty.

'The woman!' screeched one driver. His scalp was so sparsely covered it looked like the creator had been in no generous mood when he worked on his hair. 'It has to be the woman. It is always the woman. Ah! Who committed the world's first sin?'

'It's the man!' a tiger-nut seller, a young girl of about nineteen, disagreed. 'Go and look at my sister. She is only sixteen and already pregnant with her second child. The man responsible for the first one disappeared as soon as he was told of it. And this second one too, he was a really nice man, till this pregnancy came. Then come and see! He too started talking strange talk. "Ah! Didn't I do it with you all the way only once?",' mimicking, '"All the other times, didn't I remove my thing before the milk came?" Then declared that no, no, no, it sure was not him responsible. So tell me – sixteen, two children, no husband, no job. I tell you. A fine reason to abandon your baby, or?'

'Then maybe both the man and the woman should be held responsible,' one male passenger in a queue contributed.

At which point the old man book-keeper, who had been seated quietly behind his worn desk all the while, said calmly:

'We don't know what exactly happened. We don't know why what happened happened. Or how. It could even be someone else beside the man and the woman who is responsible. Who knows?

Maybe even someone among us here. So don't let us begin to judge who is guilty and who is not. After all . . .'

'What? What again, oldster?' Another driver, a younger man, could no longer contain himself. 'Spare us your silly long too-known talk, OK? The issue is a straightforward one, so why beat about the bush? The woman was a prostitute who got careless, felt the baby would ruin her business, so got rid of it in the thicket. Simple. A terrible thing to do. And only a whore, a demon, a Jezebel through and through can do that.'

'Or someone none of the above,' the old man insisted calmly. 'You would be surprised at the reasons why people do things.'

'Do what things?' the second, younger, driver again. 'Old man, what you are saying is still pure nonsense. And tell me, why should we even listen to you at all? Don't we know you? In your heyday, when that constable impregnated your wife's little sister, did you wait for any whats and whys and hows? Didn't you summon your two burly sons to the barracks to mete out kangaroo justice to him there? Should I go on?'

At which point, the balding driver who had spoken first decided that the second driver was not only veering the main issue off course, but that he was also being too rude to the old man.

'What has the issue with the old man's small sister-in-law got to do with this case, my brother?' sparse hair admonished. 'Or do you want to disgrace him for the fun of it?'

The second driver was totally baffled at his fellow driver taking such a stand against him.

'You want to argue with me? OK, it wasn't for the fun of it. It was for the fun of your mother's head. If old and white-haired as he is he cannot talk any sense, shouldn't he be . . .?'

Biff! The first blow caught the younger driver full in the face. Another caught him on the nose, dazing him. But he quickly recovered, or thought he did, and unleashed a very poorly aimed retaliatory blow. It missed his intended target, the sparse-haired driver, but hit the lips of an innocent passenger who was standing close by lost in thought. The passenger swung round, shocked, confused and clutching at his bloody mouth with one hand. Why the hell had they brought him into this? And without looking, he struck back a vicious and angry blow. Where it landed he neither saw nor cared. The person he hit yelled obscenities, felt his swollen eye and also let fly a blow. So fists started flying free and fair. It was a sight to see.

◆

It was at this point that Mami Korkor, a fresh-fish hawker, emerged from the market very exhausted, and headed for home. But seeing the free-for-all fight she beat a quick retreat and used the back gate instead. It lengthened her journey home, but better that than risk an uninvited blow.

Her late arrival angered her daughter, Bibio, so when she saw her mother from a distance, she walked to meet her halfway along the path to the compound house in which they lived.

'I have been standing here waiting and waiting. Why? Didn't you want to return home today?' she snarled at her mother, who thought it best not to try to explain things at all. Then, in an even ruder manner, Bibio asked for – no, demanded – 200 cedis for a cake of soap.

'Soap for what?' Mami Korkor snapped.

'Your son and his friend, they brought me something from the rubbish dump, which I must wash,' ten-year-old Bibio, who actually looked, thought and talked like a fifteen-year-old, replied sharply.

Mami Korkor stared briefly at her daughter, helplessly wishing she could have afforded a better life for her. Bibio, for her part, made no secret of her contempt for the life she had been born into. Whenever the opportunity presented itself, she never failed to make it clear to her mother that she was to blame for their pathetic life.

'They still go scavenging on the rubbish dump? Haven't I told you not to allow them?' mother reproached daughter, and further maddened an already irate Bibio. Furious as she already was with her life, the last thing she needed was a reproach like that. And definitely not coming from the very person who bore her into her misery.

'Mami Korkor,' (this was how Bibio addressed her mother when she was in a stinky mood), 'which of the two boys did I bring into the world?'

Her mother was taken aback.

'I don't like your tone, Bibio,' she warned icily.

Bibio chuckled.

'Too bad. You should have sent me to school to learn some manners then. But since you rather let me stay home to play mother to you and your friend's sons – boys I'm only three years older than – where else can I learn my manners but in the streets?'

Mami Korkor's jaw dropped.

'And don't forget, Mami Korkor, that this very blouse I am wearing also came from the rubbish dump.'

Overwhelmed by Bibio, Mami Korkor was at a loss. Her daughter was growing up on the wrong side of the tracks, she knew. But how could she change things? She had to hawk fish from dawn to dusk to earn just enough to feed herself and her four children. They all depended on her. Not a pesewa came from their father.

But Bibio had a different view.

'Why, after making Nereley with him, when you realised how irresponsible he was, did you go ahead to make Akai, me and Nii Boi as well?'

In Bibio's mind she would always be wrong, Mami Korkor concluded. She gave her the 200 cedis.

Next morning she saw the freshly washed flowered blouse, the underwear and the cover cloth up on the washing line. They were old, but still wearable. 'Sad,' she thought, and cursed the children's father in her head. Then she picked up her tray and headed for the market.

◆

By now, the police had been inundated with information, some of which had proved useful. A couple of the newspapers too had followed up some of the leads and started their own investigations. They were coming up with various stories about the suspect's identity. Running through all the stories, though, was one common factor: the clothes the woman was last seen wearing. And when Mami Korkor heard about it, she flinched, swore thirty times, heaped insults upon Satan for bringing more trouble on to her already troubled doorstep, then summoned the cassava seller, the market's chief gossip, and confided in her that in fact the clothing everyone was talking about was at that very moment hanging on a washing line at her house.

The cassava seller lived up to her reputation. And Mami Korkor was soon surrounded by advisers of all sorts.

'Rush home and burn it,' a garden-egg seller suggested.

'And warn them not to tell anyone,' the salt seller added.

'No!' the okra seller begged to differ. 'Send it back to the rubbish dump.'

But Mami Korkor did what her own head told her to do. She got her son, his friend and Bibio, gathered up the clothes, and headed for the police station.

A girl, sixteen or thereabouts, was seated in front of the officer in charge, chewing at her nails. She did not speak the Ga dialect in which Mami Korkor spoke to the officer, but she clearly suspected what was going on.

After the officer had taken down Mami Korkor's statement, he summoned a secretary to have it typed, and said, 'We appreciate your coming, madam. We are definitely getting somewhere. And now, let me introduce you to this young lady here.' He pointed to the girl. 'This is Akua, the one who gave us the vital clue about the clothes. She was living with a friend called Efia, who took off unceremoniously one day wearing these same clothes. And at the time she left, she was very pregnant.'

Part 2

Chapter 2

It had never been Tika's dream still to be single and childless at the ripe old age of thirty-five. Living only with Efia, her maid, in a two-room estate house, and travelling frequently all over Africa to scout for goods to sell in Ghana, was not much fun. Neither was hopping into bed with men of all shapes and sizes for the flimsiest of business excuses. But fate, it seemed, had determined it – from the day several years back when she had fallen in love for the very first time. She had invested so much of herself in this love that when it turned sour she swore to herself 'Never again!', and switched her emotions into neutral.

He was Owuraku, and they were both eighteen when they met. They had also both just completed their fifth-form secondary education and were anxiously awaiting the outcome of their Ordinary-level exams. It was love at first sight. But when the results came, Owuraku had passed with distinction and qualified for the sixth form, while Tika had failed miserably.

'Will you re-sit?' a concerned Owuraku asked.

'No!' Tika replied unperturbed.

Her mind was on her mother.

◆

Madam Sekyiwa, Tika's mother, was 100 per cent illiterate, stinking rich and riddled with guilt. At the age of twenty-two she began a clandestine affair with a married man twenty-four years her senior. His wife was barren and rumour had it that this was the result of an abortion she had had when they were courting. Then Sekyiwa got pregnant. And the man felt his obligation to his unborn child transcending his loyalty to his wife.

He left her.

'I will live the rest of my life for you and our child,' he promised Sekyiwa. 'I will set you up in business. I will make you rich. I will invest every pesewa that crosses my hand in you. So that one day, when I am old and no longer working, you can take care of me and our child.'

So, soon after Tika's birth, he got Sekyiwa a big shop and filled it with textile prints. By the third year, Sekyiwa had become one of the wealthy market mummies. Young, good-looking male gold-diggers began to vie for her attention. Her husband's libido was waning anyway, so she gave in. She gave them good money; they gave her good sex. Life's satisfaction shone in her eyes. Her husband mistook it for love; his heart was bursting with affection for his young wife.

He took her in his arms. 'Now that we have achieved what we set out to,' he looked her tenderly in the eyes, 'we can begin to really enjoy life.'

But to his dismay, Sekyiwa gave him a scornful jeer.

'Enjoy what life? What life is there to enjoy with a dead penis?'

That was how the squabbles started. No day passed without a fight or an argument. And little Tika witnessed it all.

Then one day something happened. Tika returned from school and found the house in tumult. Everyone was wearing black and crying. Her mother called her aside, explained to her what death was, and told her that her father was dead.

Little Tika remembered the fights and arguments she had witnessed between her parents. All the screaming and yelling had come from her mother; the imploring and pleading from her father. She remembered her mother's hands flying at her father's face in time with her insults. It was her father who had wept. After one such argument, her mother had stormed past her and out of the house, without so much as a glance, as Tika leaned confused against the corridor wall. She had gone to find her father and ask why he was weeping. He had cuddled her, managed a weak smile and assured her that he had not been crying, but she knew that he was not telling her the truth.

'Did Mama beat you?' she had asked.

'No,' her father had replied calmly. And as if drawing on his daughter's strength to prevent his breaking down, he had hugged her tightly and held her close. Tika had never needed to be told that her father was a very sad man.

It had been even more glaringly clear on those free Saturdays when her mother had not taken her to the shop. On such days her father had become a completely different person, playing and laughing with her. All it had taken was the sound of her mother's arrival for the gaiety to halt abruptly, as if the light of her father's life had been extinguished by the flick of a switch.

Her mother, explaining death to her, now said that her father had gone to heaven and wouldn't be returning. Tika wondered if her mother had sent him to heaven because she didn't want him any more. 'Did you make him die?' she asked her mother innocently.

Sekyiwa was stunned. 'How can you say that?' she reproached guardedly.

'Sometimes you made him cry,' Tika said.

Sekyiwa was overwhelmed.

'You are too young to understand how your father died, Tika,' she managed, 'but one day, when you are old enough to understand, I will explain to you. All right?'

Tika nodded. Then, as if seeking emphasis, she added, 'So Dada won't come back again?'

'No,' Sekyiwa replied.

'Who will play with me on Saturdays if you can't take me to the shop?'

'I will find somebody.'

'Why can't you play with me?'

'Because I have to make money to look after us.'

'So when you finish making money, will you play with me?'

But before Sekyiwa could answer that, she was summoned to talk to the new house-help she wanted to employ to look after Tika. Little Tika continued to wait and hope for the day her mother would finish making money and come to play with her.

Years later, Tika learnt that two days before her father had died, he had tried for a reconciliation with his first wife. But his ex had been greatly offended by this move and hurled every insult under the sun at him. And she hadn't stopped there.

'Bury any shred of hope you have for a possible reconciliation down a million-mile pit!' she had said. 'And make sure too that for as long as both of us live, you never cross my way or step on my shadow. Even when you were functioning down there, did I ask you back when you left me for your chicken soup? How much more now that you are nothing but a miserable piece of potato!'

She had cursed him with leprosy, should he defy her warnings, and had broken six raw eggs at his feet to solicit the powers of the gods to see it through. It had proved too much for his heart.

Tika did not blame her stepmother. Instead, all she saw in her mind's eye were Sekyiwa's hands and insults flying at her father's face.

'If you hadn't jilted him, would he have gone t reconciliation?'

So Sekyiwa had always known that Tika blamed her for the death of her father. She tried to buy her forgiveness. Tika saw her mother's turmoil and relished it. Somehow, her mother's desperation for her forgiveness eased the memory of the grave sadness in her father's face when she saw him for the last time. She gleefully accepted every financial bargain Sekyiwa offered her. What else could she get from her mother, she asked herself? And when Tika failed her exams, she knew that all she needed to do was to come up with a business proposal and Sekyiwa would finance it. For her part, Sekyiwa saw in Tika's exams bungle another opportunity to show her concern; it was a chance to purchase her daughter's forgiveness. So she decided that she wouldn't wait for Tika to ask. She would offer her help spontaneously for better effect. One morning she woke her daughter with a proposal.

'I want to set you up in business.'

'A shop?' Tika asked.

'No. But I'll get you a warehouse. You will bring in goods from neighbouring countries. Shop owners will buy wholesale from you.'

Sekyiwa asked a friend who was already in the business to coach Tika in the basics. Then she signed Tika a fat cheque as capital.

'So now am I forgiven?' she asked when she handed it over.

Tika looked at the cheque, then at her mother, and mumbled something. Sekyiwa continued to stare at her expectantly. When Tika still said nothing Sekyiwa's heart sank. What else could she do? If this generosity had also failed to make an impact on Tika, then maybe the best thing to do was to sit back and wait for Tika herself to decide when to forgive her. Sekyiwa rested her guilt.

◆

Obsessed with proving her success in spite of her academic failure, especially to Owuraku, Tika invested all in her business – her brains, her energies, her dignity. And she succeeded. By the time Owuraku had finished with the sixth form and was going on to university Tika was providing for all his needs.

'Lucky you!' his jealous mates teased at first.

It swelled Owuraku's ego.

Then it reached the ears of Owuraku's friends that Owuraku was unknowingly paying a price for his good luck. He was having to share Tika with other men, something they were certain he had no idea about. And they were no longer so jealous of him. In fact, they decided to let him in on it. After all, what were friends for? They summoned Owuraku.

'Man!' one patted him on the back. 'The way your woman has become your provider, she could be hijacking your manhood, while you have no control over her womanhood at all! Dig? Nothing is for free, or?'

Before Owuraku could work out what he was saying and make a reply, a second friend snapped to the first, 'No roundabout talk, man! Be direct!' And facing Owuraku he said bluntly, 'There is talk about your woman. Dig? Bad talk!'

'Like what?' Owuraku asked.

'Like . . .'

And Owuraku listened in pain to the gossip about Tika that everyone, except him, it seemed, had heard. He also noticed the glee with which his friends told him.

Later, stunned, furious, and feeling both degraded and humiliated, he went to look for Tika. He found her totally worn out, slumped in an armchair, having just returned from a round of her debtors. Owuraku launched straight into an attack.

'What is this ugly talk about you bedding them all? Shop owners, bank managers, customs officers?'

He thought Tika would break down and beg for forgiveness. Instead she snapped defensively, 'Do I poke my nose into your studying methods?'

Tika was overwhelmed by events. How come these things never stayed under wraps, she wondered to herself? In fact, until she got into it, she had not realised that business could entail so much unpleasantness. It took her a while to understand that in order to stay in business and perform well, she had to consent. And she needed to perform well because she wanted to prove, to Owuraku especially, that her failure had ended with her exams. For example, when she first started in business, Tika used to think that women who imported goods to sell in Ghana paid all their customs duties to the letter. Sekyiwa's friend, who had coached her in the business, had said nothing to disillusion her. It was only when she got into it that Tika realised profits made on imports were negligible if all customs duties were paid to the last pesewa. Some customs officers accepted cash bribes in exchange for reduced tariffs, but this did not apply to Samuel, the chief customs officer at the border, when the businesswoman involved happened to be young and pretty. He turned down Tika's cash offer and indicated lewdly that what he wanted from her was sex. She needed his help, so she consented.

There were others too, but how could she have explained that to Owuraku? Other women's husbands just closed their ears and minds to it. Business was business. Period. For what would happen if they interfered and the women stopped their antics, the business went down and the cash stopped flowing? But Owuraku was not like these other men. He was a university undergraduate with pride and prospects. For Owuraku, money was good, but not at any price. And that was a point Tika had missed.

Owuraku decided on an exit plan. In his heart he was finished with Tika, but he decided that he would not tell her immediately. He would leave her to think the affair was still on, and continue to benefit from her financially for as long as it would take her to realise that it was over between them. Next, he picked a girlfriend from campus. When Tika heard about it, she refused to believe it and confronted Owuraku. He did not deny it. But Tika still would not give up. It was a reaction against the pain she had caused him, she told herself. She initiated an investigation into her rival's background, learnt that she was from a poor family, and convinced herself even more that things would sort themselves out given time. Owuraku would realise that the girl had nothing to offer him.

'How can she even try to step into my shoes? What has she to offer Owuraku? Money is the power word. Not books.' And she showered Owuraku with even more cash and gifts.

'That should make him drop that "mistake"!' she assured herself.

But Owuraku sensed her frustration. And he was also still seething. So he vengefully accepted all she gave him – and passed some on to his poor campus lover.

Judgement day came when he graduated.

'When will you let your people come to see my people to perform the marriages rites?' Tika asked.

'When I find a job and save enough to finance the dowry,' Owuraku replied.

'Why wait that long? I'll provide the cash,' Tika offered.

'Outrageous!' Owuraku snarled, feigning shock. 'Only a shameless, desperate woman who wanted a husband for the sake of earning the title of a married woman would do that. Have you incinerated all your pride and dignity?'

Tika suspected vengeance.

'Are you deliberately insulting me?'

'How can I?' Owuraku gibed. 'How dare I? But believe me, my people always say a woman like that is never worth her salt. You don't buy wifehood – you earn it.'

Tika needed no further insults. She gave up Owuraku and settled on four useful 'steady' lovers. Samuel, the son of an apostolic pastor, was her customs officer on the Ghana-Togo border. Riad, the half-caste, was a shop owner with several outlets. And through Eric, the struggling musician, she remained on the favoured customers list of the commercial bank headed by his older brother. But it was Mr Attui, the factory owner, who helped her get good credit rates on the goods she bought, who proved to be her one error.

Samuel, Riad and Eric all had a wife each, wore wedding bands, talked proudly about their wives and children, and wanted only lust from Tika. Attui, however, had two wives, with a total of twelve children between them, and two concubines. He was always insulting his wives, dropped the two concubines when he met Tika, and made no bones about his desire to marry more women and add to his children.

'It is a great honour when a man dies and in his obituary you read "Widows". And when the names of all his children go on a line or two, where's the glory in that? Ten lines – that is something!'

For some reason Attui felt that Tika was hoping to become his third wife one day.

'Just keep giving it to me good,' he would moan during their love-making. Lost in ecstasy, he would insult his wives as stupid old women with dull bodies.

Then Tika got pregnant.

Whose was it?

She made some calculations and decided it must be Attui's.

'I need money for an abortion,' she told him.

'You are pregnant? Good God, Tika! No! No abortion. I'll make you my third wife. Heh? Happy?'

An appalled Tika was even more put off by the memory of her own parents' marriage. She did not love Attui and she knew too well what kind of a wife she would be to him should she get stuck with him in a loveless marriage. Sekyiwa flinging her hands at her father's face was still a vivid image in her mind. She did not want to become like her mother.

'Keep your money, Attui. I don't need it. But from now on, keep your distance. And forget you ever made love to me.'

Attui was shocked. Then he got desperate. How could he let Tika go? Gosh, where else could he get such good sex? He turned to Tika's mother, Sekyiwa, and desperately solicited her help to convince Tika to change her mind. Sekyiwa actually despised Attui. Attui did not know this because Sekyiwa was very nice to him whenever he called on Tika. But Sekyiwa decided to talk to Tika for a different reason.

'Attui came to me yesterday,' she began. 'About your condition. But my concern is not about his marriage proposal. You are not getting younger, child. Your business has become the focus of your life, so you have held other important things at bay. And I worry about you waking up one day only to realise that it is too late to do other things.'

'Like what?'

'Like having children. Tika, please, I urge you, keep this pregnancy. Like me, it may be the only one God is willing to give you. We'll care for it together. We don't need a man. I'll cut down on my business activities and be there for this child. Me and you, we seem to be just accumulating wealth without thinking who we will give it to.'

Tika thought about her late father. And about Kataso, the poor farming village in the east from which he had come. Like most villages in Ghana it had lost its most successful sons to the cities, and these sons didn't return too often to help those they had left behind. No one to give her money to?

'Wrong, mother. I have been thinking. I'll give it to the people of Kataso,' she taunted.

For Sekyiwa this confirmed the wisdom of what she had felt all along. She could never buy Tika's forgiveness. It would have to come from Tika herself.

'Go and line their roads with your wealth!' Tika went on. 'After all, didn't it come from one of their illustrious sons? I won't keep this pregnancy, mother. It will make me do to Attui's wives what you did to father's first wife. And what if it grows to be to me what I have become to you? I know you are not proud of me. I am no blessing to you. I don't only blame you for the loss of my father. Inside here,' pointing to her heart, 'I blame you for the loss of Owuraku too. You brought me up to value money above all else. So you see, Owuraku and I could have been married by now – and producing the grandchildren you crave for so desperately.'

'I shouldn't have interfered,' Sekyiwa told Tika, 'I should have known how very unqualified I am to even suggest anything to you. But, yes, I am desperate for a grandchild. So I am still begging you. Please reconsider aborting this baby. I beg you.'

But Tika did not reconsider. She ended the pregnancy.

Sekyiwa was devastated. 'You selfish, egoistic, self-centred child!' she said bitterly. 'I will no longer be haunted by what I did or did not do to you. You say I am a murderess for jilting a man who also jilted someone else? What should I call you too, heh? I paid my price to you, child. In full. Whatever price is left for me to pay must be to God my creator.'

That night in bed Tika decided it was time to move out of her mother's house.

Chapter 3

Kataso.

Her father would call her to sit beside him on the living-room couch, his legs stretched out on the coffee table, and say with passion, 'That is where my umbilical cord was buried, Tika. So when I die, please take me back there.'

While this was happening Sekyiwa would be away in a hotel room, playing a game of passion of her own – with a young lover.

Kataso, a village in the eastern hills, had no flowing water, no electricity, no entertainment centre, nothing. Only the chief owned a television set – old, black and white, and 100 per cent out of order. There would have been no power to run it, even if it had worked. It stood in the palace for decoration. A privileged few, who could occasionally afford batteries, owned pre-set radios, the kind imported from China in the 1960s; they were set permanently to the only radio station that had been available at the time.

Which therefore left sex as the only really affordable entertainment in Kataso. Everyone – young, old, mature and immature – indulged in it freely, making the two midwives the busiest of the village professionals.

The young men, when they could no longer stand this bland, grey life, would leave for Accra, Kumasi and Takoradi, to work as shoe-shine boys, truck pushers or hawkers of items such as popcorn, dog chains and air fresheners along the cities' busiest streets. Occasionally, some were booted out, on the chief's orders, for gross misdemeanour. One dawn, the palace announcer would shout out, 'Hear, oh hear, you good people of Kataso. The chief has asked me to bring this message to you all. Kofi Akorti has been asked to leave this village immediately. Mama Ama Mbroo reported that he had impregnated her fourteen-year-old daughter. This brings to twelve the young girls Kofi Akorti has so far impregnated in Kataso. The chief thinks it is in the interest of the village that Akorti carries his wilful and undisciplined penis away from here before he impregnates another twelve girls.'

The girls, in contrast, were sent for by relations or contacts in the cities to work as housemaids and babysitters, though many eventually ended up as iced-water sellers and prostitutes.

One day, four years ago, Akua, frustrated and itching to leave Kataso, but seeing no prospect at all of being sent for, did what only one girl before her had done. She left home and headed out, saying nothing to anyone.

Her mother thought she was going to friends. Those who saw her heading towards the outskirts of Kataso assumed she had been sent.

So Akua walked on, left Kataso, continued through Braha, the next village, arrived at Osiadan, and walked through town to position herself on the Accra-Kumasi highway, armed only with her determination to make it to the city.

For nearly three hours she stood by the roadside asking for a lift. Eventually a contractor's truck stopped for her.

'Where to?' the driver asked curtly.

'Kumasi.'

'You have the money to pay me?'

'No.'

He grunted. 'So you won't pay me?'

Akua unbuttoned her blouse. The driver's eyes blazed with

consent. She removed her pants. He grinned, and stopped the truck in a secluded bend.

'But don't make me pregnant,' Akua cautioned.

'I won't,' and he covered her nipples with his lips. He sucked and fondled her body. Akua liked it and did the same for him. When it was over, the rest of the journey continued in stunned silence. The driver dropped her at the railway station four hours later.

'I'm sure you'll find help here,' he assured her. And drove away.

Akua did. There were many young girls here working as porters, who had bolted from home to seek greener pastures, just like her.

'Where I come from, when two women are quarrelling, do you know how they insult each other? "Who told you you can compare yourself to me? How many of your children are in the city?" So when I told my mother I wanted to leave, she immediately gave me her blessing,' one girl revealed.

And another: 'It's the same palaver where I come from. I hear when my mother received the thermos flask and lantern I sent her last month, half the village called on her to have a look and make comparisons.' To sighs.

It was a month following Akua's arrival. She had grown more settled in her porter's job and had become more open and cordial with her friends. So she also had something to say: 'As for Kataso, the ultimate is when the city-dwellers return for the yam festival. The household with the most returnees gets the most honours and attention. And as for the dance at the Quebec Inn . . .'

'What is that?' someone asked.

'A dance and entertainment hall at Osiadan. The dance that crowns the festival is called "showtime", because that's when returnees put on their best clothes and compete with each other. I can't believe that this year I will be one of them.'

And for the rest of the day Akua couldn't get her mind off it.

What could she get her people? For her grandmother, definitely a colourful plastic chamberpot and a made-in-China enema pump. But her mother? What could she get her? Maybe . . .

'Hey, Akua! Wake up! Can't you see your customer there?' someone screamed, butting into her reverie.

She sprang up. If she was going to satisfy her people back home, then, God knows, she needed every cedi. And she rushed to help the woman who came by every week to buy eggs for sale at Nkawkaw. She spent the next forty minutes carrying the delicate crates into the train, and got a fat tip. When she joined her mates, her attention was still on the egg woman.

'What's the matter? Was she mean to you today?' one girl asked.

'Why?' said Akua absent-mindedly.

'You're staring at her with a funny look on your face.'

'Not her. Her rasta braid. Isn't it wonderful? That's what I'll wear for the Kataso festival!'

Life as a porter in Kumasi was not what a normal person would call living. It was survival. But Akua knew that, come the yam festival, the adulation she would receive in Kataso would make all her sweat and humiliation sweet.

Like her mates, Akua had no regular home. They all lived in unfinished buildings; when final completion work started, they moved out. Thanks to bribes of cash and sex, workers at the building sites regularly tipped them on the next place available for occupation. Because they were living there illegally and the building owners occasionally stopped by, nothing that might betray their presence was allowed. Cooking was out; they ate strictly by the roadside. Water stored in reservoirs for construction work sufficed for their washing and bathing purposes. Drinking water was bought and stored in plastic bottles, and nearby bushes were their easing grounds.

This is what it took for Akua to qualify as one of the soon-to-be-envied – a returnee.

At home for the festival that first year, Akua dazzled her people with tales of traffic lights, fly-overs, the latest cars on the streets and exotic events such as visiting foreign musicians. And finally, when it got to 'showtime', she joined the crowd of returnees to Osiadan proudly. The girls glowed in their outlandish kaba styles and the young men looked hip in their starched jeans, thick-soled boots and second-hand T-shirts, sporting slogans like 'Chicago Bulls' and 'Wacko Jacko', with weird lop-sided haircuts to crown it all.

'My granddaughter!' Akua's grandmother beamed with pride as she stood in her simple doorway watching her.

On her second visit home for the festival, Akua was sweating it out on the dance floor with a guy in a grey T-shirt. On the front, in bold red letters, it said 'I'm insured by the Mafia'; on the back 'If you hit me they hit you'. That's when she spotted Efia. They had been playmates as children, but on her previous visit Akua had not seen her. Efia was looking pathetic, entering the Quebec Inn in an old crumpled dress and holding two peeled oranges. When Akua called to her, she shrieked.

'Is that really you? There's no way I would have recognised you. You've completely changed!' And she went on to compliment Akua on how pretty she was and what beautiful clothes she was wearing.

'What do you do?' Akua asked.

'I sell oranges outside,' Efia replied.

Akua bought her a whole bottle of Coca Cola.

Efia was thrilled. 'I also want to come to the city,' she confided.

'Then come,' Akua urged.

'I will. Unless something happens,' Efia declared.

She sounded very determined.

Chapter 4

Something did happen.

Among the few Katasoans in Accra with formal jobs and the comfort of a home, one of whom had been Tika's father, was a lady called Teacher by virtue of her profession. And she got to where she did because she was adopted by a relation who was married to a man from Accra. Initially she had intended Teacher to come and live with her as a maid, but her kind-hearted husband saw the little girl's potential and told his wife that he wanted to enrol her in school.

'Are you not hoping for too much?' the woman asked her husband. 'The girl is almost eleven, and the children you want her to join in Class One are six to seven years old. Not only will she not fit in, they won't even accept her.'

But they accepted her.

'She is just over seven,' the husband lied straight-faced to the school head.

The head chuckled cynically. 'Of course,' she said. 'And you too look just a little over twelve!' giving him a do-you-take-me-for-a-fool glare.

But the husband came prepared.

'I understand your scepticism,' he assented, 'but it's a problem in their bloodline. Back in their village, because of their size, there is a joke that their grandfather once plucked a coconut just standing on a kitchen stool. The brother after her is just a little over six . . . but I'll call him in so you can see what I mean.'

The boy in question was the son of a friend, and twelve years old. The head gave him a dubious look.

'Must truly run in the family,' she grumbled. And admitted the child.

'Class mother!' her schoolmates mocked.

'School madam!' her teachers teased.

But, encouraged by her foster father, the girl stayed on and succeeded in making it all the way to teacher training college.

After graduation, she stayed on in Accra to teach. She maintained her links with Kataso, visiting once a month at least and joining in the yam festival every year. If Kataso could have exploited Teacher's acquired knowledge to the full and rewarded her fairly for it, perhaps she would even have returned to the village permanently. She was fifteen when Tika was born, and her feelings for Kataso never waned. This was because, like Tika's father, she had been born inside a traditional midwife's hut in the village, and her umbilical cord had been placed in a calabash and buried by her grandmother in the brown earth of the village. Tika, in contrast, was delivered in a hospital in the city and had had her umbilical cord flushed down into the sewerage system with countless others.

Because of her position, Teacher was often given the task of getting young girls from Kataso positions as housemaids with families in Accra. Usually, a guarantee was given that, after the girl had served for four years, her training as a dressmaker or hairdresser would be sponsored. As a result Teacher was very well known among the Accra Katasoans, Tika included. Before Tika was born, Teacher had known her father and his first wife, who also happened to come from Kataso. And, like most of the city Katasoans, she had also followed with keen interest the rumour and gossip surrounding the story of how Tika's father jilted his first wife for Sekyiwa, who was not from Kataso. Teacher's allegiance, of course, was to the first of the two wives. Like many of the villagers, with whom she discussed these developments, when this first wife spurned Tika's father's attempts at reconciliation, she supported her more. When the man died as a result of her snobbery, Teacher and all the Katasoans, just like Tika, blamed Sekyiwa rather than his first wife.

'Not coming from Kataso is one thing,' she said, 'but causing the death of one of her sons, and the heartbreak of one of her daughters, is another. Kataso can never forgive her.' But she did not despise Tika because of the simple fact that she had the blood of Kataso flowing in her veins.

However, on that hot, humid day, when the school messenger came to her in the classroom to tell her that she was wanted in the staff visitors' room, and she entered to find Tika, she quickly decided that there must have been a misunderstanding somewhere. Tika, realising how baffled she was, did not even give her the chance to say hello.

'I came to see about a maid. I need one. Someone from my father's family. That is why I am here.'

Teacher could not quite trust her legs. She found a seat.

'Can I sit down too, please? I feel quite exhausted,' Tika asked.

Teacher uttered a hasty apology and beckoned Tika to a seat.

'I don't think anyone in Kataso would want a daughter of theirs to come to serve and live with your mother. No matter how desperately they would want the opportunity for their daughter to escape the village, it would stain that family. They would always have to live with the guilt and shame of having given in to an enemy.'

Tika began to feel a little faint. She had been all right when she set off. The wooziness had begun on the way, but she had decided to come anyway and get the matter over with. Teacher's bluntness made clear how much ill-feeling there was in Kataso towards Sekyiwa, and it seemed to make the faintness worse.

'The girl will not be serving my mother,' Tika found her voice. 'She will be living with me. And I am on my own now.'

It was welcome news for Teacher, but, damn, someone might still raise hell!

'There are many young girls walking the streets here in Accra, who would gladly jump at the opportunity for a good roof over their heads, and the guarantee of a square meal a day at least.'

'That's true', Tika acceded, 'but I want the person to be from my father's extended family.'

Her persistence puzzled Teacher.

'Why?' she asked.

'Because I consider it my obligation that if I am fortunate enough to find myself in the position of bettering someone's life, then that person ought to be from my father's bloodline. That way, I would, in my own small way, be paying back some of what my mother owes my late father.'

That did it!

'All right!' Teacher, deeply moved, agreed. 'I'll help. I'll leave for Kataso this weekend and see the extended family.'

Tika got up, beaming with thanks, and offered Teacher her hand. Teacher took it and gave a little smile.

'You'll hear from me as soon as I return,' she assured her. But as she spoke she noticed something was wrong.

Tika suddenly went wide-eyed and stood still, staring blankly at Teacher. She was sweating profusely.

'What's . . .?' Teacher began, but in a moment, Tika groaned and was doubled up in pain.

Teacher, shocked and confused, shouted for help at the top of her voice. Minutes later, Tika was being rushed to the emergency unit of the general hospital.

◆

Since the day she had come home to find Tika gone, Sekyiwa had been living in a daze.

'Why work so hard and save, save, save? Who am I doing this for?' And she locked herself up in her house.

Initially she toyed with the idea of embarking on a wild and unending sexual spree, but, oddly enough, the idea did not appeal to her. So she tried pretending that what was happening did not bother her. But the more she did this, the more her obsession to win Tika's forgiveness grew.

'The dead cannot forgive. But if the forgiving heart of the living is big and generous enough, it can cater for that of the dead too.'

She was desperate to gain the forgiveness of her late husband too. So she continued to lock herself indoors with her thoughts.

On the afternoon of this day, she was engrossed in her thoughts as usual, and did not notice at first that someone was knocking on her front door. When she opened it, the visitor identified himself as a male nurse from the general hospital.

'Sorry, madam, but I have bad news for you,' he began, and told Sekyiwa about Tika's admission. It did not rock Sekyiwa. She remained calm and composed, which was not what the man had expected. When he heard what she had to say, he was even more amazed.

'It's good of you to come and inform me, young man, but I don't think my daughter would want me by her sickbed. Did she specifically ask you to come and tell me?'

'No. It was the lady who accompanied her to the hospital.' And it dawned on him that the lady had not even disclosed her identity to him. Sekyiwa wondered who it could have been.

The young man shrugged. 'Don't know, but she begged me, directed me here and gave me money for transport.'

'And what is wrong with my daughter?'

'Com . . . complications.'

'What complications?'

The nurse indicated his abdomen.

'The abortion?'

It hit the nurse like a bolt from the blue. 'You know about it?'

Sekyiwa smiled wryly.

'Her womb also had to be removed because it was very badly infected,' the nurse added slowly.

Something died inside Sekyiwa.

'God, why? Why did you let this happen to her? She is so young!'

The young man felt silly and helpless.

'I must be going now,' he announced.

He could still hear Sekyiwa mumbling to herself as he walked away.

◆

At the hospital, Teacher was telling Tika, 'I am making the trip to Kataso. You will need the maid even sooner now.'

And Tika was nodding weakly, and saying, 'Whatever it will cost.'

It was early in the morning on Tika's third day of admission. She had been told she would be staying a week.

'If I charter a return taxi from Osiadan to Kataso, I should be back and giving you some feedback this time tomorrow.'

◆

Teacher returned with feedback, but it was not pleasing to Tika's ears.

'Convincing them to comply took time, tact and energy,' Teacher disclosed. 'I even quoted you. They have someone ready for you, but they refused to let me bring her right away.'

'Why?'

They insisted on direct negotiations with you. I think it's just an excuse to meet you in person. You can understand their curiosity, or?'

Tika understood it. But she also needed her maid fast. 'A day or two after I'm discharged, I think we should find a taxi with good shocks and charter it straight from here to Kataso and back,' she suggested.

Teacher knew it would cost a fortune. But it wasn't her headache, it was Tika's, and what was a fortune to her was probably nothing to Tika. So, using a driver who worked the Accra-Osiadan route, she relayed a message to Kataso about the scheduled day.

'Will I have to present something? A bottle of schnapps, perhaps?' Tika asked.

'I think they prefer some loaves of bread,' Teacher advised.

◆

At Kataso on the appointed day, even though it was not even approaching noon, Efia's father was already drunk and fast asleep on a wicker mat inside the hut.

'Akpeteshie,' moaned Efia's mother. 'It's what he rinses his mouth with first thing every morning.'

'Can he join us?' Efia's grandmother, her mother's mother, asked.

The mother went to check. He was lying spreadeagled on the

floor, oblivious to the flies buzzing in and out of his open mouth, and snoring as if tomorrow were doomsday.

'He can't,' she told the old lady, who snorted angrily.

'So what do we do?' the grandmother demanded.

'Maybe we should call in someone from the family house. Papa Kaawire is there.'

So Efia was sent to call Papa Kaawire, who promptly agreed and returned with her.

When they were seated, the villagers welcomed the city-dwellers, and the city-dwellers thanked them and presented their loaves of bread. Then Teacher set the ball rolling, going over their mission again. Efia's people went to one side and put their heads together as if they were hearing everything for the first time. When they rejoined the others, Papa Kaawire spoke, his eyes fixed on Tika.

'We know what we want from you for our child. So can you also tell us what you want for yourself from her?'

'I travel a lot,' Tika began, 'so I need her to be honest and reliable, because the whole house will be in her complete care on many occasions. It is important for me to be able to trust her enough not to have to worry about my home when I'm away.'

'And chores?' Efia's mother asked.

'The basics. If she can clean, wash, sweep and cook well, that's it,' Teacher replied.

'But I won't tolerate stealing,' Tika chipped in, 'and whatever goes on in the house must remain within its four walls.'

'Understandable,' Papa Kaawire remarked, and cast a brief look at all the faces around him. He continued, 'So now can we also know how you intend to reward our child for her services?'

Eyes widened with interest.

'I will take complete care of her. I will not maltreat her. After four years, I will enrol her as an apprentice seamstress. And before we part ways she will have her own sewing machine, plus ample money to get started in life.'

Efia's people, who kept nodding throughout, declared that they were satisfied with the pledges.

'I will also talk to my daughter,' the mother began, 'to tell her to behave well. She is hardworking by nature, so I'll pray she stays that way. Her father will be told everything when he wakes up.'

'And if he happens to disagree with something?' Teacher asked.

'Something like what?' the grandmother spat. 'If he had wanted his views taken into consideration, shouldn't he have been up and with us, instead of in the sorry state he's in now?'

Efia's mother mumbled a protest, but the grandmother just gave her a rude look and pursed her lips in defiance. But the issue jolted Papa Kaawire. He placed his lips to Efia's mother's ears. She nodded and wordlessly left the group.

'I want her to check if her husband can join us now,' Papa Kaawire informed the rest.

But Efia's father was still sprawled where they had left him, still snoring, and had even more flies feasting greedily inside his mouth. Papa Kaawire was not at all pleased with that. He consulted the grandmother, then addressed Tika and Teacher.

'I know you had expected to take Efia with you, but I don't feel right about releasing her to you without her father's blessing.'

Teacher frowned. 'In other words?'

'In other words, either you wait for him to get up, or you leave money for the Osiadan driver to bring her to you tomorrow.'

Tika and Teacher consulted between themselves and decided on the latter.

◆

Efia's father woke up in the afternoon and instantly howled for his food. His wife dashed into the hut to assure him that it was coming. Minutes later he was seated and feasting contentedly on boiled cocoyam with pepper and smoked tilapia. His wife cleared the things when he had finished, then gave him water to wash his hands, and some to drink. Then she calmly informed him that Efia was due to leave the next day for Accra. The man swelled with anger, yelled obscenities, and hurled the bowl of water at his wife.

'What one reason can you have for daring to keep me out of the negotiations?' he bellowed. 'Why the hell didn't you call me?'

'I did. But you were beyond waking up.' His wife, used to his moods, was unperturbed.

'Then why didn't you let them wait for me to wake up?'

'You think a little too much of yourself, my lord. These are city people. Very busy. They would not have tolerated such a demand.'

'They wouldn't have?' He was truly flabbergasted.

His wife studied him pityingly. 'Just be grateful that we have one less mouth to feed, my lord.' And she left him.

Papa Kaawire then summoned him and briefed him in detail on what had transpired, confident that with the deal to train Efia in a profession clearly made, her father would be more than happy. Instead, after listening attentively, not interrupting once, and even nodding eagerly at some points in agreement, he asked calculatingly, 'So what's in it for us?'

Efia's mother gasped in disgust. 'I don't get you,' she managed, just keeping her patience.

Her husband stared her directly in the face and said, 'I was talking about us, her parents. What are we getting out of our daughter's going away to the city to serve somebody?'

Now his wife flared up. 'Why are you talking as if we were

selling our daughter? Is this like her getting married? Where we should be entitled to some dowry?'

'No?'

'No, for God's sake! The lady, in spite of who she is, sounded like a good person. And Teacher would never have agreed to bring her to us if she wasn't sure of her. She's going to do something that we could never have done for our child. Be grateful for that at least.'

But Efia's father was even more astonished that his wife was not seeing eye to eye with him.

'Didn't we take care of her up to this stage? And if we hadn't fed her up to now, would she have grown strong enough to be able to serve her?'

Efia's mother exploded, 'That was our responsibility, or? We did no one a favour feeding our own child, or?'

But her husband was not going to be upstaged. 'You prepared well for a confrontation, eh?'

Silence.

'And she leaves tomorrow, you said?'

'Yes.'

The ensuing atmosphere was tense, and heavy with suspicion and suspense.

◆

Moments later, Efia's mother went looking for the old lady. 'Mother, we don't have enough cassava for this evening's fufu. I have to go and uproot some more,' she told her. And left for the farm.

On her return, a very atypical scene confronted her. Her husband and mother were locked in an intense tête-à-tête. The two were like fire and water. They never greeted each other, and at the least opportunity she would scream 'Useless!' at him and he would scream 'Witch!' at her. So what on earth had they found in common to warrant such close communication?

She found out in the middle of the night, when the old lady woke her up, and asked her to wake Efia as well, for an important discussion.

The grandmother addressed Efia, 'Your father gave me the surprise of my life yesterday. He proved to me that though his body has fallen to akpeteshie, his brains have not.'

Efia's mother began to fidget nervously. What the hell was coming next? She soon found out.

'He drew my attention to something I had previously not considered at all,' the old lady went on. 'We simply discussed it. But the sensible man that he has proved to be, he left it to me and my old wisdom to actually initiate things. And I tell you, our beloved ancestors did not let me down.'

Efia's mother was by now so dumbstruck that she could only stare as the old lady turned to address her.

'My child, Teacher's choice of Efia for that Tika' (Efia's mother winced: 'that Tika'?) 'was due to the good work of the ghost of Tika's father.'

'That Tika' was bad enough, but ghosts? 'What are you trying to say, mother?'

'Of all the extended family members, why did Teacher settle on us? She could have gone to the family house, or? Look at all the girls cramped in there just waiting for an opportunity like this. Yet Teacher took just one look at our Efia and decided she was the one. Why? Because the ghost chose someone who could hear and understand his distant voice – me. Through your husband. The way that evil wife hurried Tika's father so prematurely to his grave, I tell you, his ghost will never find rest till he settles his score.'

Efia's mother was stunned. 'Ei! Mother!'

But the old lady ignored her. 'Listen, the ghost wants to return to his family all that his evil wife stole from him. The money that Tika used to start her business, wasn't it part of her mother's blood money?'

Efia's mother couldn't help but agree.

'Good! And now, believe me, the money is destined to return to this family,' with finality.

'My mother's gone mad!' Efia's mother thought to herself. Then she asked, 'What is it you want to tell us, mother?'

The old lady seemed to be proving how mad she was. She turned to Efia, 'Listen! The woman you are going to live with is a rich but wasted woman.'

'Mother!'

'A very wasted woman.'

'Mother, please!'

'An unproductive womb is bad enough. But no womb at all? And that is what she is. A walking woman with no womb inside her . . .'

'God, mother! Really, you must be . . .'

'So, my granddaughter, if you ask me, the present circumstances are no coincidence at all. It has been destined this way ever since that day that evil wife stole our illustrious son's . . .'

'Please, mother . . .'

'The gods and ancestors of this village of ours designed everything. And your going to live with her is an essential piece of that design. So hear me! Be subservient, humble and very dependable . . .'

'Good advice, mother!'

'Then get yourself pregnant.'

'W-h-a-a-t?'

'You both heard me right. Efia, you will live with her, win her affection, become indispensable to her. So that when you innocently become pregnant . . .'

'Innocently? How does she become pregnant innocently?' Efia's mother asked.

'By pretending she was forced into the sexual act,' the old lady replied.

'By whom?' the mother again.

'It doesn't matter. Hers is just to get pregnant.'

'How?' asked Efia innocently.

'Fool! By sleeping with a man. How else?' her mother yelled, warming to the old lady's plan, whatever it was. 'Don't tell me you don't already know about that!'

The old lady cast her daughter a curious look and smiled a little. Then she turned back to her granddaughter. 'On second thoughts,' she began, 'when you get pregnant, refuse to name the father.'

'Why?' Efia's mother's interest was intensifying.

'Because it will save us the risk of some foolish man getting up one day to lay claim to the child after it has become the somebody it will surely become. And this is the plan. Inevitably, that Tika will rush to inform us of what has happened. And that is where I shall also play my part. Old and wrinkled as I am, when I bombard her with the volumes of tears I shall shed, she will need an iron heart to turn down my fervent plea to forgive my granddaughter. I will sob like a child, go down on my weak old knees and beg her to have mercy on us.'

'It should work!' Efia's mother enthused. 'But you do know what you are doing, mother, or?'

'Of course, child!' And she knew she had won her daughter over.

'In the midst of my tears,' she went on, 'at the right moment, I will turn the tables. I will suggest that maybe all this happened with the blessings of our ancestors. And emphasise how her dear father too is now one of our beloved ancestors.'

'Ooh! Mother!'

'Then press home my point that my instincts tell me it is the wish of the ancestors to bring the joy of a crying baby into her life.'

'Oh, mother!'

'And offer her Efia's unborn child.'

Efia and her mother went dead quiet.

'I will urge her, in my low shaky voice, to adopt the child, make it hers.' And she paused for effect.

'That's it?' Efia's mother could not contain her curiosity.

The old lady gave a long deep laugh. 'And to think your husband and I were worried you wouldn't agree . . .'

'Oh, mother!' embarrassed.

'But no, that is *not* it. That is how the wealth will return to us.'

'How?'

'Child!' admonishingly, 'Do I have to tell you everything? If she makes that baby her child, what do you suppose will happen if she dies? Or even before then? And who do you think will eventually inherit her wealth?'

'Oh, mother!'

'So I am happy that we are all in agreement now. It means success is assured. Our task will be to make sure that the child never forgets who her real mother is. That way, the wealth will also belong to Efia, and therefore to us all. And we will let it trickle down and spread. We will transform Kataso. The village will hold us in great estimation. May our ancestors see us through!' with dogged determination.

'Oh, mother!' admiringly.

'Oh, grandmother!' shyly.

Chapter 5

Efia followed her grandmother's counsel to the letter. And Tika could hardly hold back her elation.

'She is too much!' she told Teacher.

And Teacher said, 'Well, then thank God.' And was truly grateful that the Almighty had yet again guided her to make a good and trouble-free choice. 'It improves my own reputation too, or?'

Tika agreed, but did not tell Teacher that the situation was making it tough and uncomfortable for her in matters to do with her many men. Efia had proved herself very dependable, running the house with a master hand. But, perhaps even because of this, Tika did not know how to fit her into that other life of hers. Diplomatically, she told Efia that the men who regularly called on her were business partners. That, of course, was not entirely false, but Efia was no fool. Madam's female business partners always ended up in the living-room.

'Efia, bring us some beer and glasses. We have a lot to thrash out,' madam would say.

But when the partner was male, it was, 'Efia, make sure Mr —— and I don't get disturbed. We have a lot of business to discuss.' And Tika would disappear with him into the bedroom. Next thing, the key would turn in the lock. And the many times that Efia placed her ear to the keyhole, she heard noises: moans, groans, pants and sighs, and the wild creaking of the bed.

'What does that have to do with business discussions?' she thought. 'Who does madam think I am?'

So one day, when a certain business partner called on madam and they ended up behind the locked door of the bedroom, and a second business partner then came knocking on the front door, Efia's quick instincts propelled her into taking the greatest risk she had ever taken in her housekeeping career. She took one look at the man at the door, thought about the business transaction already taking place in madam's bedroom, and said to him, 'Madam should have returned from Lagos yesterday, but she sent a message about an unexpected hold-up and said she would be back tomorrow.'

The man frowned. 'And this car?', pointing with suspicion at the dark blue Toyota Carina parked in front of the house.

'It's madam's mother's car. She often comes around to check on things when madam is away. She is fast asleep now, but if you want me to wake . . .'

'No!' the man snarled, appalled. 'Of course not!' (thinking 'Twerp! What do I need the mother for?') 'Here is my card. Make sure she gets it as soon as she returns.' And he turned, took a final look at the blue Carina and walked to his own car.

Hours later, when Tika had ended her dealings with partner number one and had seen him off to his car, Efia summoned all her God-given courage and told Tika what she had done. Tika knitted her brows. 'The girl might damn well be telling me she knows what sort of transactions go on behind my locked door,' she thought to herself.

'What are you trying . . .' but she cut herself short, her face clearing. Yes, why not? Was this not the problem solving itself? If Efia had made the first move towards knowing and understanding, why not make her a party to the deals?

That was how it began. In cases of bad timing or sheer bad luck, when an imminent clash loomed, or if Tika did not want to see a particular partner at a particular time, Efia would diligently take it upon herself to persuade the man in question, whoever he was, to please go and come back another day, because 'Madam is not back,' or 'Madam's uncle is visiting from the village', or, as happened on two occasions, 'Madam is very sick, so a pastor is with her at the moment, praying'.

It all turned out so fine. So perfect.

'Oh, Efia! What would I do without you?' Tika asked. And she told Teacher, 'I'd be lost without her.'

It was as if everything were under a wonderful spell.

◆

Then, one day, the spell was broken.

Tika was getting ready to do a round of her debtors, and called Efia to instruct her about food for the day.

'I'll be back in the evening, so cook the rice around 3 p.m. But prepare the stew right away. The meat has been out of the freezer too long.'

Efia nodded obediently and reminded her that Mr —— had said that he would be coming around 8 p.m.

'I'll be home long before then,' Tika disclosed.

'Around what time, madam? Just in case . . .'

'By 6 p.m.' And left.

Tika could easily afford a very good second-hand car in fine condition, but the idea never caught on with her. Being away from home a lot would necessarily mean employing a driver.

'Houseboys and maids, drivers and maids, garden boys and maids – they were always hopping into bed with one another. No way!'

Plus, a driver about the house would also mean another pair of inquisitive eyes peering over her shoulder. No thank you.

So, as usual, on this day, Tika chartered a taxi, and directed the driver to her first debtor. The driver watched her back disappear into the debtor's shop, adjusted his seat into the reclining position, then closed his eyes and prayed that his lady passenger would hire him for the whole day.

'Look at me, praying for my luck to shine, so that I can make some money off a woman. These market mummies are taking over the country. They dazzle you with their monkey humility, wheedle all your money out of you, then aim for your power. I bet . . .'

But his musing was rudely interrupted.

'Open up, driver! Open up!'

It was his lady passenger knocking frantically on the taxi window.

'I left something important at home. Hurry! Take me back quickly, or I can't finish my rounds today.'

And when the driver took off, he asked, 'Money?'

'Sort of. It's my record book. When I don't have it, they argue with me about their debts.'

The driver saw his chance to impress his passenger and, with luck, get hired for the day. So he drove like a bat out of hell. He had barely stopped in front of the house when Tika was out and dashing to her front door.

'Dashing for money. Dashing for power. The ultimate control!' And he noticed as he spoke that all was not going too well for his passenger at her front door.

◆

He was right.

Tika stood there shuddering with rage, as she desperately tried the knob a second time.

Damn! Why was it locked? Efia never locked the front door when she was inside. This could only mean that she was out. But where? She should be in, preparing the meat stew. Why had she left the house?

And Tika tried the door again. But still no luck. She put her bag on the balustrade and searched for her own bunch of keys. She hardly ever used them. They were the spares of all the keys in the house and the warehouse. Gosh, how alike they all looked! Which one opened the front door? Why did she never pay attention? Finally, she settled on one.

'Luck, luck, please be on my side.' She inserted the key. It clearly wasn't the right one, but that wasn't the cause of the confusion on Tika's face. There was already a key in the other side of the lock.

'The door is locked from the inside. That's it! What the hell is going on?'

'Efia!' she shouted.

Silence.

'Efia!!'

Silence. She banged on the door in rage and fury. There was still only silence.

She made to bang on the door again, then stopped. She could hear some shuffling inside. She put her ear to the door and heard muffled voices. What the hell was going on? She banged again.

'I know you are in there, so open up, Efia!' she bawled.

Efia responded slowly, 'Please, madam, I am coming.'

Tika's ear was still pressed to the door, and just as she heard Efia speak, she also heard the kitchen back door slam shut. Fuelled by suspicion, she dashed to the back of the house, but there was nothing there. No one.

She rushed back to the front door, and there was Efia, unruffled and unflustered, standing in the doorway like chastity in person.

'Can you tell me what was going on in here?' Tika demanded angrily.

'Nothing, madam,' Efia answered, like an angel.

Tika was beside herself with rage. 'Don't you dare madam me so monkey-politely! Do I look like a fool to you? Who were you mumbling to inside just now?'

'No one, madam.' She spoke so impassively, Tika fumed even more.

'You were in here with somebody doing God knows what, and you made whoever it was leave by the back door before you let me in. Isn't that it?'

'No, madam.'

A helpless and defeated Tika was raging at fever pitch. 'How do I handle this?' she thought. 'What am I to do? And how long has this thing been going on? God! The girl sometimes has this house to herself for a whole week. What goes on then? And yet, how can I get on without her?'

'I have no option but to report this to your people,' Tika said. 'I must let them know that I cannot tolerate situations like this.' She went into her bedroom for the book, which she found on the bed. 'God! After all that, I nearly forgot you again.'

As she made to leave, she stopped by the door and said, 'I am off again, Efia. So you can continue whatever it was you were doing from where you left off.'

Efia didn't flinch, and that enraged Tika. 'I think I'll even go by the station and send a message to your family. I'll want to meet them soon.'

Tika felt confident that she had played her trump card. 'She must be stewing inside with fear by now,' she thought. 'This is ridiculous. Didn't she come to work for me? Who said she could come and copy what I do?'

◆

But while Tika sat speeding towards town in her taxi, thinking these thoughts, Efia was doubled up in the house, clutching her belly and laughing her guts out.

'"Get ready to meet your people",' she mimicked, roaring with even more laughter. At last she shouted towards Tika's bedroom door, 'She's gone. Come out!'

The guy who emerged from under Tika's bed looked so petrified, Efia convulsed with giggles again.

The guy was bemused. 'I could have been caught. She could have looked under the bed and seen me.'

'No,' a dauntless Efia said confidently, 'because before I opened the front door, I banged the back door. So she thought I let you out before I let her in.'

The guy was truly impressed. 'And to think I always thought of you as naïve. Ei!'

Efia started to undress. 'She won't come back till this evening. Let's do it again.'

'But what if she does come back?' the guy asked nervously.

'Stop asking questions and let's get going,' Efia rebuked, 'and when your milk is coming don't remove your thing.'

The guy's mind was already on the cheap pornographic film he had watched the day before at the rundown video centre next to the public toilets. He had no time for any whys.

Chapter 6

Teacher listened in complete silence, dumbstruck.

'So you think she was in there with a man?' she asked Tika.

Tika affirmed she had no doubt in her mind that that was the case. Which left Teacher very upset. She always felt very strongly about the maids she introduced to people for the simple reason that if the maid were no trouble, it enhanced her reputation in the city. And when the city people kept their promises and sponsored the maids to learn a trade, it improved her image in Kataso. Teacher was no good Samaritan as such. Not only did she enjoy the fringe benefits that came with her efforts, she actually looked forward to them. As people say, 'A good reputation is fine, but you can't buy with it in the market.' So in came the cassavas and plantains and bushmeat from grateful Katasoan families. And in came materials, provisions and cash from happy city people, Tika included. Therefore for Teacher, this Efia issue was a personal crusade.

'Let me establish the truth before we decide what to do,' she entreated Tika.

And Tika revealed that the next two months were going to be busy for her anyway, as she had trips to Togo, Lagos and Abidjan to make. 'It should give you plenty of time and ample breathing space.'

Fortunately Teacher knew other people in the housing estate where Tika lived; she had arranged maids for two families nearby.

And from these maids she learnt that the guys in the area had nicknamed Efia 'Cheap Chop'.

By the time Tika had returned from her trips abroad, Teacher had arrived at a decision.

'Let's send for her people.'

◆

Efia's mother was busy pounding her palm-nut for soup. She raised her head just in time to see one of the Osiadan station errand boys heading towards her.

'Efia!' her instincts told her.

She received the message without summoning her husband. She headed straight to the old lady afterwards, a big grin on her face.

'This must be it!' the old lady exclaimed, thrilled. 'Ooh! My granddaughter!' And she hugged Efia's mother.

Mother and daughter held on to each other, dreaming dreams and thinking thoughts, until Efia's mother released herself from the old lady's embrace and asked brightly, 'So when do we go?'

'Not when do *we* go. When do *you* go?' the old lady stressed.

Efia's mother was alarmed. 'When do *I* go? Mother! Are you shifting everything on to me now that it has happened?'

'Silly you,' she gibed, 'it's part of the plan.' And sat down. 'Early tomorrow morning you will set off for Accra. She sent us money for the fare, or?'

'Yes.'

'Good. So you will go to that Tika tomorrow. And when she tells you the news, be shocked . . .'

'Like this?' making a face. They both laughed.

'Yes,' the old lady resumed, 'she must see you very shocked and distressed. Maybe you should even do something to prove it. Yes! Slap her!'

'Who?'

'Efia, of course. Who else? Tika? So give Efia a few sharp slaps. And be overcome with emotion.'

'Should I shed tears?'

'That would be wonderful. But what if the tears refuse to flow?'

'I'll tie some ground pepper in a small cloth and rub it into my eyes. She won't see.'

'Wonderful! Rub it well into your eyes and cry like a child. Then say what has happened is too much for you to deal with alone, so you must return here to consult.'

'All right.'

'But promise to return in two days.'

'I should?'

'Yes. And this time, I will return with you.'

'Oh, mother!' Hugs, hugs and more hugs.

'And now go and finish the soup. I am going to see your husband. He can be talked to, or?'

'Yes. He didn't go to Kill-Me-Quick. He drank just the quarter bottle under his bed.'

◆

The following day, when Tika saw the mood in which Efia's mother arrived, her heart went out to her immediately. 'How can I ever send Tika back?' she thought. 'It will kill this woman.' And she welcomed her.

But as Tika explained what had happened, she noticed Efia's mother's initial melancholy give way to chagrin. 'Doesn't she believe me?' she wondered.

For her part, Efia's mother was so disappointed that she couldn't contain herself. 'That's it?' she shot out rudely.

Tika frowned, not believing her ears. 'Do I take that to be your way of telling me that what your daughter did wasn't bad enough?'

The iciness in Tika's voice jolted Efia's mother. 'No! Madam Tika, please, that's not what I meant. I mean, oh . . .' and she sprang up. 'Stupid girl!' she screamed at Efia, who all this while had been standing there quietly and looking on helplessly. 'Is that what you did?'

And at a loss as to what else to do, she swiftly administered six slaps across the cheeks of a very bewildered Efia, who could not understand why she was being beaten for something she had been ordered to do.

'But mother! . . .' she started to protest.

'Shut up!' her mother cut her short. 'Not one word from you, hear me? Not one word!' And she meted out two more slaps.

Efia was stupefied. 'Mother! But . . .'

'Please!' Tika interceded, unknowingly saving the situation. 'Please don't hit her again.'

Tika should have heard Efia's mother's inward sigh of relief. Out loud Efia's mother said, 'It's not all right, Madam Tika. She deserves to be hit. Foolish girl! You wait till your father and grandmother hear about it!'

At which point Tika declared that it really was enough. 'This is her first time, Maame Amoakona, so please let it go. Moreover, now that she knows I will not hesitate to inform you if she repeats it, I am sure she won't even dare to again.'

Panting with rage induced by her disappointment, Efia's mother snapped, 'The better for her.' And slumped back in her cushioned seat. ('How soft, how comfortable, how pleasurable!' she thought. 'When, oh when?') And she yelled, 'Get out of my sight!' at Efia, who strode timidly away, completely stunned.

Maame Amoakona then turned to Tika to offer belated apologies. But Tika stopped her, expressed her own regrets about the situation, and invited her to stay the night.

'The day is too far gone. And it might get dark even before you reach Osiadan.'

('Soft bed. City food. A chance to explain things to my poor Efia,' Maame Amoakona thought.) 'I thank you very much, Madam Tika. You are kind. Thank you.' And rubbed more pepper into her eyes.

'Don't cry, Maame Amoakona, please. Efia!'

'Madam!'

'Come and show your mother to your room. She is staying the night.'

'Thank God,' Efia thought, and cast her mother a look that could kill.

'I'm going out,' Tika declared. 'I'll also go by Teacher's and tell her all is now settled. Maame Amoakona, have a good rest. And you, Efia, the stew; remember we are now three.'

'Yes, madam.'

◆

Efia stood there, heart pounding, waiting anxiously for Tika's back to disappear, so that she could devour her mother alive. Her mother also knew what was going on inside her daughter's head, so she did not wait for her to pounce.

'It was all just for show,' she explained as Efia gave her a dagger look. 'I had to act upset.' And she showed her the small cloth with the pepper.

Efia understood.

'And now, tell me, the one you were hoping would make you pregnant, was he the one you were nearly caught with?'

'He already has, mother.'

'He has already done it with you?'

'He has already made me pregnant.'

'He has? Ooh! Efia! Ooh . . .' She stopped abruptly. 'What makes you think he already has?'

'In the two months madam travelled, I didn't see my blood.'

'Ooh! Efia! And to think I was so disappointed. Come. Sit down. Let's think. No, you go and do your work in the kitchen. Leave the thinking to me.'

◆

By the time Tika returned, Maame Amoakona had figured out what to do.

'Madam Tika,' she began, 'the shame my daughter has brought on us is great. When I return to Kataso tomorrow, I will make a full report. Her grandmother may want to come to . . .'

'No!' Tika cut in sharply, horrified. ('Damn! They want to jump on this case to make this their second home.') 'Maame Amoakona, this is no case at all to warrant a visit by the old lady, is it? So please let's not drag it out.'

Efia's mother smiled. 'You have proved again what a kind woman you are, Madam Tika. Thank you. And, believe me, the way I have dressed her down, I doubt she will look a man in the face again.'

Tika sighed with relief. 'Just as long as you stay away,' she thought.

In the morning she packed some old clothes into a carton for Efia's mother to take to Kataso. Maame Amaokona thanked her lucky stars, but not because of the old clothes.

'Madam Tika, please can I seek your permission to have Efia help me to the station with the box of clothes?'

'Of course. Oh, Maame Amoakona, why? Do you have to beg me for that too?'

On the way to the station, Efia's mother said to her, 'I had to get you to come with me so that when I return here with your grandmother the day after tomorrow, I will claim that you only confessed your pregnancy to me at the station. I will say I was so affected by it that I couldn't even summon the courage to return with you to tell her. And that I proceeded to Kataso to tell your grandmother.'

'So you and grandmother will be back?'

'Yes. The day after tomorrow.'

'All right.'

'And if you receive more slaps, remember it's for show.'

Chapter 7

Tika was standing on her porch, staring into space and thinking about three things in order of importance: the algae growing in the cracks of the cemented floor ('This requires patchwork and repainting. I hate the green greens'); her mother, whom she had neither seen nor talked to again, since she moved out ('What is she doing with herself? Still sleeping around like a teenager? Now that I am out of her house, she probably won't even bother taking them to motels. And that is a house she once shared with my dear father'); and her men ('I guess I should be calling it quits soon with Samuel. Kumi, at the other entry point, is happy with cash bribes. Riad is still useful. . . . Will anything ever change? For better? For w . . .').

'For worse,' she muttered to herself, as she saw two approaching figures in the distance. 'Bloody, bloody hell,' she thought. 'What, again?' And as Efia's mother and grandmother came nearer and their very grim faces became more apparent, she decided it must be bad news. She received them with an apology.

'Sorry if I look taken aback, but you must understand that I was certainly not expecting you.' And she invited them into the living-room.

When they sat down, the old lady's head refused to stay still. All her life she had lived in Kataso. The nearest she had come to town life was Osiadan. This was her first time in the big city, and her first time inside a well-furnished room. And it was fascinating. She greedily feasted her eyes on the elegant furnishings. Tika, observing her askance, thought 'Witch!', and directed Efia to bring them water.

Efia filled two cups with ice-cold water, and came and served them. Her mother gulped hers down with glee. She had developed a liking for the iced water. In the intense heat, it was cooling to her throat. But the old lady had only half her teeth left. The effect on her weak gums was therefore not so welcome. She took one sip, spat it out on to the carpet, clenched what teeth remained, and held her jaw in pain.

'Why,' she screamed, 'do you want to uproot the rest of my teeth from my mouth? Wicked child! Unmerciful rat!'

Tika's mouth fell open. Why was the old lady being so rough with her grandchild? But Efia's mother saw through it quickly. Her mother was taking advantage of the situation to demonstrate anger at Efia. It hadn't been planned, but it was a help to their cause.

'Mother, you could just have said it was too cold for you,' Efia's mother reproved. And she rose to wipe the carpet with her cover cloth.

Tika shrieked in horror and quickly rose to restrain her.

'How can you do that, Maame Amoakona? It's only a carpet.' And helped her back to her seat.

Efia's mother sighed heavily. 'We are all just so edgy, you know, because of the matter on our hands. Oh God!' She buried her head in her palms.

Tika grew tense. 'If whatever it is has to be said, why not let us just say it?'

'Madam Tika,' the old lady joined in, 'something terrible has happened.'

'Why? Is someone dead?' Tika asked, keyed up.

'No,' Efia's mother replied. 'It's worse.'

'What could be worse than death?' Tika asked.

'For poor people like us, sometimes certain situations can be worse than death. And in situations like that, death sometimes turns out to be more of a relief than a loss.'

Tika began to sweat. 'This can't be good,' she thought.

'Madam Tika,' Efia's mother resumed, 'two days ago while I was here, something struck me. I confronted Efia about it but she vehemently denied it. Then . . .'

The old lady felt her daughter was wasting time. 'Madam Tika, Efia is pregnant.'

You could have heard a pin drop.

'It was only at the station that she finally told me. And, Madam Tika, believe me, I called upon the gods to let me die there and then. "Efia, what is this you have done to us?" I asked her. But all she did was cry.'

'And didn't you say she said that the person who did it to her forced her?' the old lady prompted.

'Oh, yes. Yes! She told me that just as my vehicle left. He forced her.'

'Who?' Tika managed.

'She refuses to say. But when my daughter arrived at Kataso and I saw her eyes – ask her – I screamed. I said, "Amoakona, why? Have you gone and fought with someone?" They were so swollen.'

'I couldn't stop myself. I cried from Accra to Osiadan and to Kataso. What else could I have done, eh?' And she sniffed, sniffed, sniffed.

'She didn't return to tell you about it because she was so afraid,' the old lady came in again.

'And she still hasn't said who is responsible?'

'No!' the old lady replied.

Tika frowned. And called out to Efia who crept timidly into the room. She confirmed that all that had been said was true.

'And will you tell us who did it?'

Efia shook her head.

'Madam Tika,' the old lady began, sliding from her seat to kneel before Tika.

Tika was petrified. 'What are you doing? Please get up.' And she tried to help the old lady back on to her seat.

By now the grandmother was engulfed in tears. 'We are poor people,' she began. 'You helped us greatly by coming for Efia. And now this. So why shouldn't I cry?'

And before Tika could say anything, Efia's mother was on her knees as well, wailing and cursing Efia. She held on to Tika's leg tightly.

Tika struggled frantically to free herself. 'Maame Amoakona, leave me! I said, let go of my leg!' But to no avail.

'Madam Tika, please, in the name of the great Almighty God, and for the sake of our ancestors, please don't abandon our daughter. Have mercy on us. Have pity on us. What can we do for her? Look at us. Look at her father. You saw everything for yourself, didn't you? Oh God!' And still she sniffed, sniffed, sniffed.

The old lady wondered what part of the plan this was, and gave her daughter a bemused but impressed look.

'Madam Tika,' Efia's mother proceeded, 'please don't send Efia back to us. Please! And when she delivers, too, please, the baby is yours. We are donating it to you. Please!'

'Yes, Madam Tika, listen to the voice of an old woman. My grandchild is yours. Keep her. And when she delivers, my great grandchild is yours too. It was God-sent, believe me. The gods and ancestors also willed it. It is your child.'

Tika was so overwhelmed that she yearned for Teacher desperately. She stared blankly at all the faces, sighed and said, 'I will think carefully about it. But I want you to leave tomorrow morning, the two of you. Efia can remain till I decide what to do.'

◆

That night in their room, grandmother congratulated mother, and mother congratulated grandmother. In undertones.

'I never knew you could shed so many tears, mother. You didn't cry half so much when father died, or?'

'And why should I have? The man had . . . how many were we? Sometimes even I lose count!'

'You were five, mother.'

'Yes, excluding the concubines. And what did he leave me when he died? Troubles and more troubles.'

'Oh, mother!'

'I tell you, when I die and go up there, do you know what I'll tell God? That when he sends us back to earth, he should let me and your father marry again. Only this time I'll be the husband and he can be the wife.'

'Oh, mother!'

Laughter.

'Oh, grandmother!'

More laughter. In low tones.

So far so good. What could go wrong?

'Just make sure you don't talk more than you should,' Efia was warned.

'What if Auntie Teacher tries to force me to talk?' Efia asked.

'Don't talk all the same.'

'And don't worry. We will be in close touch.'

Chapter 8

Tika was drinking beer and Teacher a Bluna Tropic, and they were seated at the Crabs-Do-Not-Bear-Birds spot.

'Some things don't fit,' Tika declared suddenly, waking Teacher from her daydream.

'What things?'

'Like I told you, the mother said Efia confessed to her at the station. When I called Efia and asked who was responsible, it was the grandmother who promptly alleged Efia was refusing to name the man. See?'

'See what?'

'Look . . .'

'I am looking,' said Teacher with a cynical chuckle, trying to sound light-hearted but failing. How was all this going to rebound on her?

'See, it was me who saw them first, when they arrived. They only saw Efia when I summoned her into the living-room. And all the while, not once did I leave the three of them alone. To make sure, I asked off-handedly whether Efia was still refusing to name the man. And I stressed the "still". And guess who promptly replied again? The grandmother.'

Teacher looked thoughtful.

'So when was it that they asked her again? How did they know that Efia still refused to name him?'

'Well, maybe . . .'

Teacher could come up with nothing.

'So, you see?'

'Yes. They are hiding something. They probably sent someone to Efia the day before, behind your back, to drill her.'

'Or maybe Efia mentioned the name to her mother at the station. But for reasons best known to themselves, they don't want me to know.'

'Whatever it is, I think the sooner you wash your hands of her, the better. These villagers can sometimes be fiendish. And this matter could get complicated.'

Tika agreed with Teacher on that. But then she also needed a maid, and couldn't do without one.

Teacher promised to secure a new one for her fast. 'The sooner the better. I'll go to Kataso on Friday to scout around.'

Tika parted with money for the purpose.

◆

It was the second Saturday following the Friday on which Teacher had travelled to Kataso to find a new maid for Tika. And when Efia's father left for Kill-Me-Quick, it was not to argue, it was to booze till kingdom come. But his first drink proved too light for his taste and led to rocky upheaval.

'That quarter you just served me, it was part water!' he accused the akpeteshie seller.

The seller was offended. 'How long have you been drinking here? When did I ever serve you anything bad?' she shot back. 'Pitiful liar!'

'I never lie,' Efia's father retorted. 'Not about that!' pointing to the drink. 'And upon the ugly face of that witch of a mother-in-law of mine, who now thinks I deserve her daughter after all, I swear that that first quarter was diluted.'

The seller decided to ignore him. Let the drunk talk and talk until he was tired. But another tippler, who felt that no akpeteshie in the country ever matched that of Kill-Me-Quick, concluded that Efia's father was just being too knowing. 'Don't you think that maybe your mouth is full of grass, which was why it tasted diluted?' he charged.

Efia's father was piqued. 'You filthy scum,' he scorned. 'At least none of my daughters has produced six children with six different men.' He expected a further attack from the man but, to his consternation, the other drinker roared with laughter, clutching his belly, and flinging his arms and feet wildly in the air.

'Mighty Jehovah! Look who's talking?' And he grabbed his belly again, infecting others with his laughter. 'Have you also heard of any of my daughters leaving grandly for the city, only to be faced with the prospect of getting sent back for having gone to . . .' he said, with a wiggle of his hips.

Efia's father frowned, confused. 'What kind of insult is that?' he asked.

But the man only convulsed with even more laughter. 'Look at you!' he sneered. 'You are so drunk you don't even remember your own problems. Foolish man! Coming to talk nonsense to me!'

'Me, a foolish man? So I can't remember my problems, eh? Wasn't I just talking about my mother-in-law?'

The truth finally dawned on his opponent. So he made a face, feigning sympathy, and yelled, 'Colleagues! The poor man has not heard!'

Efia's father searched the faces in bewilderment, understanding nothing.

'That daughter of yours who left for the city, haven't you heard that she has gone and . . .' gyrating his hips, '. . . and bam! Caught the ball! Gooooaaaaal!' To wild hilarity.

Efia's father hastily downed the rest of the drink in his glass, grabbed what was left in the bottle, wrapped it in his cloth, and left the group amidst jeers and laughter. He had known Efia was pregnant, of course, but he couldn't understand how the news had leaked out. 'What the hell is going on?'

◆

Efia's little brother was hunting birds to roast for lunch with his friends, when one of them suddenly remarked, 'If your sister wanted to get pregnant, why did she go to the city? Who goes to the city to get pregnant?'

The boy sought further clarification, excused himself and rushed home to inform his grandmother.

◆

Efia's mother was returning home from the farm when a friend called to her, 'Oh Maame Amoakona, have my sympathies and give all to God, eh? But I can understand your pain. I feel it for you. Such a wasted opportunity!'

Efia's mother's face clouded with confusion. 'I don't know what you're talking about,' she said.

'Oh Maame Amoakona,' with pity, 'how long can you go on pretending? It would have been different if the city woman was keeping her. But now Auntie Teacher has come looking for a new maid for her, it means your Efia will be sent back here, or?'

And that was when the very astonished look on Efia's mother's face told the woman that she had probably not heard. 'Ei!' she grew alarmed. 'You haven't heard? Oh! Then it is true what our elders say, that the person whose neck the axe is aimed at is usually the last to see it coming. I think you'd better hurry home.' And she disappeared back inside her hut.

A very disturbed Maame Amoakona reached home to meet an even more disturbed grandmother.

'Hurry!' the old lady beckoned as soon as she set eyes on her daughter. 'Go to your husband's room and check if there is anything, something small, to pour libation.'

But Efia's mother refused to move. 'The gods and ancestors are probably displeased with us already, mother. Otherwise why would they let that Tika decide to send Efia back to us?'

'So what you are telling me is that we sit down and do nothing? Child, go and bring the drink. Whatever it is that we have done that has displeased them, I will ask them to forgive us, and entreat them to see this through for us. It will work, you'll see. So go and bring the bottle,' she urged.

Efia's mother felt helpless. She gave her mother a brief look and left reluctantly. But she returned shortly to say that there was nothing in the bottle.

'Then give me water. A calabash full,' the old lady persisted.

But Efia's mother had had it. 'If libation must be poured, then my husband should do it, mother. You are desecrating the gods and ancestors. Old though you are, you are still a woman who once menstruated. And not even menopause cleanses you enough to qualify you to pour libation. And maybe things are beginning to go wrong because you broke a few rules. Don't you agree?'

The old lady was shocked. 'You have the guts to take a stand for your husband against me? That stupid drunkard? It's his bad luck that has caused all this. I was beginning to think something better of him. Now look! And you dare tell me it's my uncleanliness to blame? Get out! Go! If he's the one you say is clean enough to pour libation, then go and call him. Go!'

And Efia's mother, baffled by the intensity of the old lady's animosity, hurried off towards Kill-Me-Quick.

The moment her back had disappeared, the old lady went for the calabash of water and slipped off to the back of the compound.

◆

Maame Amoakona met her husband heading for the house in a trance, and didn't need to be told why. Wordlessly, she turned and continued back home with him, arriving just in time to catch the old lady emerging from behind the hut holding the calabash.

'Mother!' Maame Amoakona screamed, horrified. 'You went ahead and . . .'

'I didn't!' the old lady retorted too curtly, betraying herself.

'You did what?' Efia's father yelled, realising what was amiss.

'Mind your own business!' the old lady snapped, unrepentant.

Efia's father was bloated with fury. 'I'm going behind the hut right now, you old witch, to call upon the gods to reverse whatever it was you asked of them. Do you hear me?'

But the old lady grew even more defiant. 'Go ahead!' she shot back. 'Go and pour your libation. Who says the gods will favour a drunkard over a woman?'

And in spite of Efia's mother's fervent protests, her father unfolded the half bottle of akpeteshie hidden in his cloth, snatched the calabash from his mother-in-law and headed for the back of the hut.

'The situation is only going to get worse,' Efia's mother cried.

But at dawn of the following day, much to her surprise, the old lady woke her up with a bright smile. 'Didn't I tell you that the gods would rather listen to a woman than a drunkard?' she told her daughter. 'They have shown me the way to compel that Tika to do as we wish.'

A bewildered Maame Amoakona frantically wiped the sleep from her eyes.

'Who did Efia say got her pregnant?' the old lady asked.

'She said she slept with different men: the one she was nearly caught with, the building site labourer, the lotto forecaster at the station, and the dancer at . . .'

'Dancer?'

'Yes.'

'They pay him to dance?'

'That's what she said.'

'But couldn't your daughter have chosen better men?'

'I don't recall us having advised her on that, mother.'

The old lady frowned suspiciously. 'Are you being sarcastic with me?'

'No mother,' haltingly, 'it's just that I think we shouldn't forget that everything she did was your idea.'

The old lady's face furrowed in such anger it multiplied her wrinkles a thousand-fold. 'And can you also remind me, please, what role that good-for-nothing husband of yours played? So don't try to remind me about whose idea it was, right?'

'Yes, mother.'

'And now listen to what the gods directed. Is that Tika not a known whore?'

'Mother!' taken aback. 'What now?' she wondered.

'So if Efia should claim it was one of Tika's men . . .'

'Mother!' stunned.

'Shut up and let me think! It must be someone who is married. Someone who is sensitive about his reputation. Someone who wouldn't want it to leak out that he was visiting that Tika. Because to establish the truth, questions would be asked – questions about what he was going there to do. See?'

'Oh, mother!' softening.

The old lady smiled. 'That Tika will have no choice but to keep Efia, and make my great-grandchild her child – and her future beneficiary.'

'Oh, mother!' admiringly.

'And now send someone to Osiadan. The message should reach Teacher and that Tika today; they should expect us tomorrow. Hurry!'

'Yes, mother,' reverently.

Chapter 9

The message reached Teacher just before school was closing. So she left right after school to go to Tika's, but found that she was out.

'She said she would be passing Tema,' Efia disclosed.

So Teacher left a message that Tika should call on her at her house for an important discussion if she returned early enough. But Tika did not get back until quite late, so she decided to wait until the following day to meet Teacher at her school. And when she learnt about the impending arrival of Efia's people that same morning, she scowled. 'It'll be a wasted trip, that's for sure,' she told Teacher. And she entreated her to be around if she could. Teacher promised that she would be.

Efia's mother and grandmother arrived just before noon. They found Efia alone in the house and took that as a further sign of support from the gods.

'They knew that we would need time alone with her before confronting that Tika,' the old lady declared, and promptly convened a meeting.

Efia was briefed about Tika's intention of sending her back to Kataso, something which made Efia howl in horror. The sheer thought of life back in Kataso filled her with the utmost panic.

'Will you let her do it? Send me back?' she asked her grandmother, getting hysterical.

The old lady smiled. 'My grandchild, do you know what God did next after he had created the cat with an appetite for mice? He gave the mouse a flair for dodging the cat.' And she explained her plan to Efia in detail.

Four of Tika's lovers were discussed. And, upon further scrutiny, the mantle of doom fell on Mr Nsorhwe. Nsorhwe was stout, bespectacled and the manager of a big commercial bank. He belonged to two church societies and was the chief elder in one of them. He had been married for seventeen years and had two children who were both enrolled in a very prestigious school. All in all, he was the perfect bait.

'Who said the gods were mad with us?'

◆

When Tika finished her rounds, she chartered a taxi for home, but checked her time and, on impulse, decided to pass by Teacher's place and pick her up. During the ride home, neither of them spoke. Each was occupied with her own thoughts, and it was only when they got out of the taxi outside Tika's house, that Teacher asked Tika what she would do if the women pleaded fervently with her to keep Efia.

'I certainly will not keep her,' Tika replied, 'but I will continue to care for her while she is in Kataso. And one day, when her baby is old enough to be left behind, and circumstances allow it, I might still decide to put her through her dressmaking training. Because in spite of what she has done, the fact remains that she has served me well during her short stay with me. Or?'

Teacher smiled. 'This will make your father proud,' she added.

To which Tika chuckled and said, 'If he is watching.' She beckoned Teacher into the house.

The moment they entered and saw the very relaxed manner in

which Efia's people were resting in her living-room, Tika felt anger welling up inside of her. 'They are beginning to feel very much at home here,' she thought. 'Too much at home.' But she courteously bid them welcome, and asked if Efia had offered them water.

'Oh she has,' the old lady blurted out. 'We have been here since almost noon, you know, so, as for water, we have drunk plenty.'

Tika ignored the sarcasm. 'We got the message about your coming but, as you know, business is business. And Teacher also had to go to school. So.' And very conspicuously she refused to add the apology she knew they were expecting. They were getting on her nerves.

'The reason we came,' the grandmother continued, 'is because the wind carried to our ears back in the village news of your attempt to get yourself a new maid . . .'

Both Tika and Teacher were taken completely by surprise. This was not what they had been expecting to happen.

'. . . which could only mean that, in spite of our pleas, you intend to dispatch Efia back to us. A rather unfortunate development . . .'

Tika winced.

'. . . because it left us with no choice but to press Efia and find out who was responsible for the pregnancy . . .'

'And you did?' Teacher butted in anxiously.

She was ignored.

'. . . since as you know, we are too poor to take this burden upon ourselves.'

'So?' Tika snapped, getting even more irritated.

Efia's mother took over. 'When we set off this morning, we thought we would come and meet you so that we could drill Efia together. As it is, we had to do it alone and, thank God, we got results.'

Tika should have sighed with relief, but the look on the old lady's face warned her not to. She had a hunch that something bad was coming. She began to fidget.

Teacher, realising that Tika was not going to say anything, spoke for her. 'It's fine then, isn't it? That you know who did it? It's what we all wanted, or?'

But the old lady replied brusquely, 'I *don't* think it's all that fine,' stressing the 'don't'.

Tika and Teacher exchanged worried looks.

'The man responsible,' the old lady proceeded, 'is one of your friends, Madam Tika.'

And Tika's mouth fell open. 'Me?' she howled. And instantly began to itch.

'I'm afraid so,' the old lady answered coldly. Then she turned to Efia's mother and said, 'Tell her what Efia said.'

The mother cleared her throat nervously. 'She said he was one of those business partners of yours who, whenever he came by, would disappear with you behind the locked door of your bedroom for discussions.'

A confused Teacher began to mutter some gibberish, but Tika remained unnaturally calm.

'She said the man showed up here one day to look for you, but you were away on one of your trips,' the old lady resumed. 'But he apparently came well prepared . . .'

'For what?' Tika asked sharply.

The old lady chuckled triumphantly.

'Did you come here for a confrontation?' Teacher demanded.

'Of course not. How would we dare to come and challenge you in your own home? But, according to my grandchild, the poor man, very disappointed by your absence, and too aroused to go back unsatisfied, vented his frustration on her. She said it happened so fast she didn't even have time to think about screaming for help. And the result is what we have now. So.'

'Efia!' Tika yelled, charged up.

'Madam,' Efia responded, suddenly a little scared, and entered the room timidly.

'What did you tell your people?' Tika snapped.

Silence.

'Did you make all those allegations?' Teacher howled.

Silence.

'Can't you talk?' the old lady bawled.

Efia began to stutter.

Tika grew suspicious. 'Efia,' coaxingly, 'look at me. What was it you told your mother and grandmother? Don't be afraid. Say it. Tell me.'

'It . . . it . . . was Mr . . . er . . . Nsorhwe.'

A flustered and overwrought Tika screamed, 'Nsorhwe made you pregnant? You're sure it was Nsorhwe?'

'Ye . . . yes.'

And to the astonishment of everyone, Teacher included, Tika roared with frenzied laughter.

'Shock effect,' Teacher thought. 'She is going berserk.' And aloud, 'Can I talk to you alone?' And not waiting for Tika to reply, she dragged her into the bedroom.

Efia's mother, alarmed by Tika's reaction, asked the old lady if she thought Tika was going crazy over the accusation. But the grandmother was thinking along different lines. 'Was that what her crazy laughter conveyed to you?' she asked her daughter pensively.

Just then Tika and Teacher re-entered the living-room. And when she saw them, the old lady's instincts told her that something was not right. Teacher looked so settled and calm, something she had definitely not been when they made their hasty exit into the bedroom. So what had happened in there?

It was Teacher who spoke. 'Tika wants me to tell you that she has taken note of everything and will do what must be done.'

'Yes,' Tika barged in without warning, and even Teacher was taken by surprise. 'And I also want you to know that, but for a sheer twist of fate, Ananse the spider would have taken over as king of the jungle and driven the lion to hide his shamed face in the corners of ceilings. I sincerely thank you.'

Mother and grandmother exchanged anxious looks.

'I shall inform Nsorhwe immediately,' Tika went on, unperturbed, and asked Efia again, 'You said it was Nsorhwe, or?'

And Efia fidgeted so nervously that the old lady nearly slapped her down.

'But don't worry,' Tika went on, 'so long as you are sure it is him, he will do what he must. Trust me.' And she smiled sweetly.

The old woman wanted to wipe the smile off her face. 'Child of a whore also turned whore,' she thought, and began to worry about the muddled signals of the gods. On whose side were they?

Chapter 10

When it came to sex, Nsorhwe had been with Tika only twice. Yes, he had visited the house several times, but it took a couple of such visits before Tika even deemed it useful to allow him into her bed. She needed an overdraft from his bank, and he was the man who could allow it to happen. So she shut her mind to his unsightly looks and imagined him to be someone else. Even so, when it was over, she rushed to the bathroom and threw up.

Nsorhwe was a man who was very honest with himself. In particular, he was honest about his very ugly looks. Short, plump, plain-faced, pot-bellied, square-headed, and with a pair of buttocks that would have better suited the behind of a Makola mummy, it was as if his creator was in a rotten mood when he made him. But what he lacked in looks he was more than endowed with in brains. So he sailed through school entirely on scholarships. And after graduating from the university, he earned another scholarship for further studies in Britain. All this while, however, Nsorhwe remained a virgin.

One day at the university, where his brainpower was a constant topic of discussion, he realised that he needed the touch and feel of another body against his, and it occurred to him that maybe his sharp mind could overshadow his ugliness and get him a girl. He was realistic. He knew that, high IQ and all, he would still never be able to land a prospective Miss Ghana. So he turned his attention to a second-year psychology student who was not a beauty either by most standards. One Friday afternoon after lectures, he caught up with her.

'There is a good film showing at the Club House tomorrow night. I was wondering if you would be available to go and watch it with me?'

The instant Nsorhwe spoke, the girl imagined him in the doorway of the women's hall, walking past the porter's lodge amidst the giggles of the girls who were always hanging around there and who would be wondering who the hell this very unsightly *homo sapiens* was coming to meet. And there she would be, minutes later, descending the stairs with this very disagreeable creature, leaving the hall with him to even more gibes and ridicule.

She looked Nsorhwe in the face, appalled, shrieked in sheer horror, rushed to her room and cried for three hours continuously. She knew she was plain, but she had never considered herself ugly enough to warrant Nsorhwe daring to ask her out on a date. It was the nastiest slap in the face she had experienced so far. And this is what she later told Nsorhwe in no uncertain terms. The event was the straw that broke the camel's back, destroying what little confidence Nsorhwe had with women.

'Whoever decides to be with me will undoubtedly be someone very desperate for something,' he acknowledged to himself. And left things to fate.

Years later he found his desperate bride in London. And at the same time he discovered some very unpleasant facts about himself as well.

Cherry was a very frustrated Ghanaian woman struggling to make a life in London. She cleaned toilets by day and served in a very run-down bar at night. It was the kind of bar that catered for the likes of Nsorhwe, and it was where he first caught her attention.

The daughter of a former minister of state, who had died suddenly of heart failure when a *coup d'état* saw the government in which he was serving out of power, Cherry suddenly found herself on the rough side of life. Plus she had the additional burden of an illegitimate daughter. Life was hell, and anything that could take her away from it was heaven. So when she found out that Nsorhwe was unattached, doing his masters and doctorate, and had the guarantee of a good life ahead of him back in Ghana when his studies were over, Cherry saw him as her saviour. Without further ado, she invited a rather baffled Nsorhwe to her very gloomy apartment one evening. She gave him the night of his life. Nsorhwe's head spun like crazy. In Cherry he too had found his heaven on earth. What he didn't know was that Cherry had not chosen the date of their first night at random. She had chosen a day during her fertile period, because she was hoping to trap Nsorhwe.

'Nsorhwe, something terrible has happened. I have picked seed.'

'You have? Oh, Cherry! And you call that terrible? I am happy about it. I am going to be a father.'

'And me?'

'You? You will be my wife. Do you think I'll let my child be called a bastard?'

She played this scene over and over again in her head. But though she slept with Nsorhwe often, she did not get pregnant. She grew desperate. It couldn't be her; she had a daughter to prove it. So she decided to test herself. She made plans to bump into an old flame accidentally, then made a few calculations and ended up in bed with him. The following month, bang! It happened. She gave Nsorhwe the good news, and events unfolded just as she had imagined over and over again in her head. Nsorhwe promptly proposed. They married. She bore the child. Nsorhwe officially adopted her first child. They returned to Ghana with their son and daughter. And the one-time toilet cleaner became Mrs Bank Manager with a driver to take her wherever she ordered, plus a houseboy, a housemaid and a gardener, all at her beck and call.

'We have two more to make. I want four children,' a smitten Nsorhwe told his wife.

But, of course, it did not happen. And as his son grew up, Nsorhwe began to notice that he and the boy were miles apart in looks. He secretly went through a series of tests and learnt that his sperm could never fertilise an egg. He accepted his fate honourably.

Tika found out about his condition the first day they ended up in the bedroom together. Nsorhwe too had no idea at all about Tika's hysterectomy; otherwise he would have known, when she claimed to be unprotected, that she was just putting him off.

A very aroused and desperate Nsorhwe assured her that there was nothing to worry about. 'Even if I make love to you twenty-four hours a day every day, you will never get pregnant.' And, leaving out the sordid details, he told her his two children were actually all Cherry's and that he had adopted them.

And now Tika couldn't help thinking, 'What a twist of fate! Why, of all my lovers, did they pick Nsorhwe?'

◆

'What crazy accusation is that?' an enraged Nsorhwe was bellowing in his office, banging his fist on the table, having listened shocked and flabbergasted to Efia's allegation. 'This is preposterous! Stupefying! Beyond belief!' And he choked on his breath. He held his throat in despair, coughing violently. Tika rose to his side and patted his back.

'There is no need to kill yourself over this,' she consoled.

But Nsorhwe was beyond consoling. 'No need to kill myself? That is exactly what I want to do. Do you have any idea what this will do to me? Holy Christ! I want to die. I want to bang my head against this wall and split it in two. Who in my position can live with the shame of something like that?'

Tika remained calm. 'You won't have to live with any shame, believe me.'

'Believe you? What is this, hmm?' irritated at what he perceived to be Tika's indifference. 'I am close to losing my all: my job, my position in the church, my standing in society. God! Maybe even my family too! And all you can do is tell me to believe in you?'

Tika put her arms around him. 'Calm down! I said calm down. Listen to me.' And she drew him against her. His square head rested just below her breasts. 'Horrible creature!' Tika thought, and sat him down. Then she carefully unfolded her plan to him.

But Nsorhwe only stared at her in disbelief. 'What are you saying?' he shrieked. 'What is this bizarre thing you are asking me to do? And what makes you think I would want to take a risk like that?'

'All right,' Tika snapped, 'I am trying to help. But if you don't want my help, then, sorry, but you will have to deal with this alone. And live with your shame.' And she rose to leave.

Nsorhwe grew desperate. 'Tika, please don't go. Don't leave me this way!'

'Shouldn't I? What should I do then? Stay and listen to you moan while you walk to your destruction?'

'No! No, wait. I'll do it. It's crazy, but if it's the only way out, what choice do I have?'

Tika smiled. 'So it's settled?'

'Yes, it's settled.'

'Good.' And she left to go and inform Teacher about everything. But she decided against Teacher's suggestion that she should be there too. 'This is something I must see to alone.'

◆

Early the following morning, Nsorhwe arrived and knocked on Tika's front door. Tika had by then assembled Efia's mother and grandmother in the living-room, having already briefed them that Nsorhwe was coming round for them to thrash things out. Tika observed the old lady start at the sound of the knock while the mother absent-mindedly cracked her knuckles. And she was pleased.

Both were anxious, that was clear. But they were obviously also expecting a more anxious, flustered, maybe an even more irate Nsorhwe, since the man, after all, did not only know he was innocent but also that his chief accuser knew he was innocent too. So initially they thought it couldn't be Nsorhwe who had entered the living-room. Then Tika introduced him and they were thrown completely off balance because, contrary to their expectations, Nsorhwe strode in brisk and breezy, wearing the brightest and broadest of smiles. And he very cordially shook hands with both mother and grandmother.

The old lady thought, aghast, 'Has he forgotten what he is being accused of?' She turned her attention back to Tika, who was saying smoothly, 'As I told you, Nsorhwe offered to come and meet you without delay.'

At which point Nsorhwe butted in excitedly, 'Oh yes. These things happen, you know. But, please, forgive me.'

Tika smiled apologetically. 'Efia!' she called. And Efia entered the room and stood at a respectful distance.

'Really,' Nsorhwe resumed in the same exhilarated manner, 'if you ask me, I cannot understand why Efia remained silent about it for so long.' Then he turned and faced Efia square-on with his square head and asked, 'Efia, why?'

The old lady's face creased in bewilderment. This was turning out differently from what she had expected. It was going too smoothly, it was too good to be true. What the hell was happening?

'I called on you to tell you personally that, as soon as it is established beyond doubt that this child Efia is carrying is mine, believe me, I will wholeheartedly accept it with open arms. And I will name him in one of the most elaborate ceremonies Accra has yet seen. Ooh! I can feel it in my bones that it will be a baby boy. Ooh!'

Efia's mother went so wide-eyed that for a moment it seemed as if her pupils were receding. As for the old lady, her mouth fell wide open, apparently trying to say something. But whatever it was got stuck in her throat. She began to cough like crazy.

Nsorhwe, ignoring them all, made his next move. 'I want to correct one impression, though. I never forced Efia into sex on any occasion. Never. Efia,' and he turned to face the hopelessly baffled girl, 'why did you say I forced you? Didn't it always happen with your full co-operation? And wasn't it even sometimes you who made the first move? And, tell me, why were you taking all the biscuits and chocolates if it wasn't with your consent? Please,' to Efia's thunderstruck family, 'each of the times it happened she was more than a willing partner. So I was really shocked, indeed, very offended, when I learnt that she claimed I forced her. Efia,' turning back to the perplexed girl, 'all the sixteen times it happened, do you really want your people to believe I forced you? Sixteen times?'

'Sixteen times?' Efia whispered in shock.

'Sixteen times?' mother and grandmother, completely dazed, repeated in unison.

'Earth, oh earth, open up and swallow me whole!' Efia prayed silently. And her people felt they understood nothing at all any more.

'The gods must be drunk,' thought the old lady, 'or they've gone on a break.'

It was the moment Tika was waiting for; her cue, so to speak. She rose. 'Efia! So all this was happening behind my back? After trusting you enough to leave this whole place in your hands? So you want to eat from the same plate I eat from? How many more of my men friends were you sleeping with and charging biscuits and chocolates, eh? Tell me!'

But Nsorhwe launched into a string of apologies, taking all the blame upon himself. 'Tika, forgive me, please. But try to understand. You know how my wife treats me. And you too kept spurning me. I had been starved for so long. And when I came that first time, Efia was just coming from the bathroom with only a towel around her. The thought of her nakedness underneath it made me crazy. And things just got out of hand. My mistake was that I let it continue. Please forgive me.'

But Tika glared at him and yelled that forgiveness was not the most pressing point at the moment. 'That is!' she screamed, pointing at Efia's belly.

'I know, Tika, I do. And you know me too, don't you, Tika? That I love children and never forgave my wife for not giving birth to more kids. So as soon as it is established that this child is truly mine, I shall inform my family and we will accept this child into our fold.'

Efia was suddenly overcome with dizziness and had to grab hold of the armchair for support.

'I don't like this establish . . . establish . . . talk, Mr Nsorhwe,' the old lady chimed in, fretful and beside herself with worry.

Nsorhwe chuckled. 'It's just for me to make sure the child is mine, that's all. After all, ask her,' pointing to Efia, 'whether I was the only man she was sleeping with.'

'But of what use is that now?' the old lady asked desperately. 'She has specifically named you. She is the carrier of the child, and only she knows the true father. You!'

'Sure. But it is not that simple, you know.'

'No?' Efia's mother was so nervous, Tika nearly laughed.

'Sure. Oh, come on! Did you think I would accept that I was the father just like that? Without verification? In these modern times? It is just a matter of having the usual blood tests . . .'

'Blood tests?' the old lady scowled.

'Oh, don't worry. It doesn't take long. And I also have an American doctor friend who will see to it. I shall bear all the costs. It must just be confirmed that the child is mine, that's all. I am not one to run away from my responsibility. But I am also not one to take on a responsibility that is not mine.'

'Where the hell are the gods and ancestors? Why aren't they intervening to stop this crazy turn of events?' the grandmother thought. 'So, this blood test, what is it?' the old lady asked aloud.

Nsorhwe stole a knowing glance at Tika, who was fighting with all her will against bursting into laughter.

'Actually, it can be painful, but this friend of mine . . .'

'He is a white man?'

'Yes. It is his job. That was what he was doing in America before he came to work here. So it won't take long. First he will draw some blood from my veins; then he will draw some from Efia's too. Then . . . hmm . . .' and he paused lengthily for maximum effect.

Six eyes stared at him in great suspense.

'I am sorry, but this is the part that is most painful. But it also happens to be the most important. They will have to draw some blood from the baby too.'

'How?' Efia's mother shrieked.

'It's simple. They use this special long needle with which they will pierce Efia's womb to draw the blood from the baby too, after which . . .'

'I won't do it!' Efia yelled in a frenzy.

'She's right,' said the old lady. 'Why go through such a painful test when you know already what the result will be?' And went numb.

Tika turned to the mother and grandmother.

'Mr Nsorhwe is a good man, believe me. And everything he has said he will do. So, please, I beg you, just allow him to make sure the baby is his. Because after that he will bring it up very well, and ensure it a promising future.'

'The baby is not his, fool!' the old lady wanted to scream at Tika, but she asked Nsorhwe instead, 'So this method can show whether the baby is yours or not?'

'Yes,' Nsorhwe replied. 'And I am sorry it has had to come to this, but if Efia had been faithful to me, all of this would not have been necessary.'

Mother and grandmother consulted among themselves and asked that they be given time to consider this new development. Nsorhwe also sought permission to return to the office. And Tika, who actually had nowhere in particular to go but who wanted to leave the three alone, also excused herself and left the house.

◆

'You fool, fool, fool, fool, fool!' the old lady attacked her granddaughter as soon as they were alone. 'Why of all your whore of a madam's lovers did you let us choose this little, ugly, square-headed man? Heh? You fool a thousand times over!' And she felt bad heat inside her head.

'Mother,' Efia's mother came in soberly, feeling her daughter's pain, 'all we can do now is come up with some excuse to leave here graciously with Efia.'

'Yes,' with biting cynicism, 'and disappear forever back to Kataso with our miserable failure. And now what will happen? We will be a laughing-stock. And you,' pointing to Efia's mother, 'should it get out of hand, rest assured that I will be the first to visit the chief and tell him where the idea came from. And you too,' pointing accusingly at Efia, 'better start thinking about the life waiting for you back in the village. Even without a child, how was it?'

Efia's mother, seeing the mood the old lady was in, decided it was best not to argue further. 'My husband will deal with you,' she inwardly consoled herself.

'We will leave tomorrow morning, so go and pack your things,' the old lady commanded Efia. And she strode out of the living-room on to the porch. She needed to cool her head. Suddenly not even the cushions seemed as soft as they had been.

Efia left quietly for the kitchen and slumped on to one of the stools, her mind whirring. Kataso? How could she endure the shame? She would be scorned, snubbed and ridiculed. To go to the city, mess up and return not only empty-handed but with the additional burden of an extra mouth to feed was unforgivable. How could she bear it?

Her thoughts turned to the yam festival and she squirmed. 'How can I face the more successful returnees? I certainly can't take part in the festivities.'

And on the spur of that moment, the idea struck. 'Madam Tika . . . the bedroom . . . under the wardrobe . . . the black leather bag . . .'

She rose, found a big plastic bag in the kitchen, entered her room, threw in a few things, came out and went into Tika's room.

She pulled out the black leather bag, helped herself to as much of the money as her plastic bag could carry, went back into the living-room and slipped out through the back door.

The old lady was still cooling her head on the porch. And her mother, exhausted by it all, had fallen asleep in the armchair.

Chapter 11

It was brisk and bustling as usual at Kumasi train station as the two young men from God-knows-where haggled over which of them was responsible for spilling the cooked groundnuts the twelve-year-old vendor was carrying. And while the girl stood there wailing and telling the world how her mother would kill her when she got home that day, plenty of young and hungry kids, too preoccupied with their own empty stomachs to worry about the plight of the girl, saw their manna from heaven and hungrily clamoured for the spilled groundnuts.

Akua and her friends, standing at a distance and looking on, could not help laughing.

'That'll teach that vain and foolish girl not to go insulting us free of charge. There isn't one of us who hasn't been insulted by her when we complained about the number of groundnuts she gave us,' Akua charged.

'Eh, my sister! Say it again,' a friend in red supported. 'Ah! Just because we come from the village to work here doesn't mean we should be looked down on, or?'

'Hmm,' Akua chuckled, 'the other time, when that girl's cooked eggs scattered, look at the number of us who quickly rushed to her aid to save the eggs from being filched.' To several nodding heads.

There was another loud and desperate wail from the groundnut girl.

'Eat your wails and insults!' the girl in red scorned. And, turning to Akua and the others, she said, 'I have my own problems. The owner of my base has returned from abroad and wants to resume work on his building, so I had to bribe Atinga yesterday with a couple of quick rounds behind the blue kiosk to get him to find me a new place.'

'Two rounds?' the one with the plaited hair screamed. 'Ei! Then you really tried! The time I did it, I did only one round with him, and I had to sit on hot water for two days!'

'Well,' Akua came in, 'as for me, fortunately work has been suspended on my building. I hear the owner has travelled to some country to get work and make more money to come back and complete it. So for the next year at least, neither Atinga nor any of them will see my pants.'

Just then someone yelled Akua's name. It was the tiger-nuts seller. It irritated Akua, 'My sister,' she yelled back, 'all I have made today is 1,000 cedis. How can I afford the luxury of tiger-nuts?'

But the tiger-nuts seller shook her arms angrily. 'Who said I was calling you because of tiger-nuts? It is this girl looking for you.'

'Who?'

And Efia came into full view.

'Eeeei! Efia!' and she rushed to her. 'Atuuuu!', she cried, embracing her. 'Ah, but when did you get here?'

'Just now.'

'And what are you . . .?

'Won't you welcome her properly first?' the girl in red reproached Akua.

'Welcome her here?'

'At least buy her a cup of iced water. It's better than nothing, or?'

'Oh, don't worry,' Efia came to Akua's rescue, 'I just had some. I'm full.'

'In that case, sit down,' Akua suggested, and dragged her to a nearby seat. 'And tell me what you are doing here. Did you come with your madam?'

'No.'

'She sent you?'

'No.'

'You are here by yourself?'

'Yes.'

'Why? Has something happened?'

Efia's long, worried pause confirmed Akua's worst suspicions. 'It's a long story,' she managed at last.

'Then I'll have to close a little early and go home with you. Let me make 2,000 cedis more, and then we'll go.'

◆

At Akua's place, when Efia had briefed her on her predicament, Akua got scared. 'I think you should return to Kataso,' she urged. 'Because, whatever happens, and however bad it seems, you will still be safer there than here. Look at the way we live here.'

And Efia acknowledged that, in comparison, living with Tika was a luxury. She had had a room to herself, a comfortable bed with a fine foam mattress, access to ice-cold water direct from the fridge, a gas stove to cook on, and a guaranteed breakfast, lunch and supper. Now look at her.

'I know nothing about childbirth,' Akua continued, desperate to get Efia to agree to go back. 'And I don't have the time or money to look after you.'

But how could Efia go back?

'Money is no problem,' she assured Akua, 'I have enough to see me through till I deliver and find my feet.'

A deflated Akua sighed. 'Well, that is one problem solved. But still . . . and anyway, what do you intend to do after the baby is born?'

'I will send it to my mother in Kataso, and return to Accra.'

'Which means you intend to deliver here?'

'Yes.'

Akua shuddered. 'Efia, are you sure you won't get me into some kind of trouble?'

Silence.

Akua gave up. 'All right. I'll tell the others. There are three of us here. The others work in a chop bar. If they agree, you can stay.'

◆

The others agreed to have Efia with them, as long as she did not let her presence affect their daily routine. Efia assured them that she wouldn't get in the way, and kept her word. She went nowhere, and always stayed indoors. She did nothing except sleep, wake up, bath, eat and sleep, sleep, sleep.

'Won't you start attending clinic?' a concerned Akua asked on one occasion. But Efia replied that it was not necessary.

'It *is* necessary!' Akua insisted.

But Efia wouldn't budge, and eventually confessed her fear of someone spotting her. Her worry was not so much about being spotted by someone from Kataso, but by someone who knew about the money she had stolen from Tika.

'Your friend,' one of the chop-bar girls remarked to Akua one morning, 'you'll have to insist she sees a midwife. Her stomach has stopped growing. Haven't you noticed?'

And although Akua brushed her friend's remark aside, she could not help but agree that all did not seem to be going too well with Efia's belly. Yet Efia still refused to venture out. They all prayed for her delivery day to come quickly and pass without problems, so that Efia could leave them and take her troubles away.

Their prayer, unfortunately, went unanswered.

A scream in the middle of the night, some weeks later, was the first sign of trouble. Yet when they rushed to Efia's side, there she was, awake and smiling, insisting it was just a bad dream she had had. By morning, however, she was so pale that it should have alerted the ignorant three. But they left for their various workplaces, completely unaware of what would be awaiting them on their return.

It was the two chop-bar girls who came home first. So they were the ones who met Akua halfway down the path leading to their place to tell her that Efia had disappeared. Then they led her to one of the rooms. There was so much blood in one corner that Akua screamed. 'She must have delivered,' she added flatly.

But the smaller of the chop-bar girls could not envisage the possibility of Efia having gone through it all by herself. 'Maybe when it started coming, she shouted for help and someone heard and came and helped her to the midwife.'

So off they went to the midwife. But Efia was nowhere around there.

'Let's inform Atinga,' the other girl suggested. 'Maybe she went into the bushes and is still there.'

So Atinga was informed and asked to organise the boys in a search of the bushes. But Atinga would hear nothing about it.

'Nonsense!' he bawled. 'Was I the one who put the baby inside her belly?'

So the issue of Efia had to be put temporarily to rest.

'We will just have to wait and see,' the bigger of the chop-bar girls muttered in despair.

But Akua had other worries about the matter. 'What if we never see her again till I go to the yam festival and they ask me about her?'

Then, very unexpectedly, events days later provided the answer. The news of the abandoned baby's corpse found in the thicket at Braha swept through the railway station and shook the very souls of Akua and her friends.

'Braha is quite near Osiadan,' a very thoughtful Akua remarked. And attracted a chorus, 'So?'

'The baby could have been born around the same time that Efia disappeared from here, leaving nothing but plenty of blood.'

'So?'

'It was her intention all along to send the baby to her mother in Kataso.'

'You told us that. So?'

'No bus goes directly to Kataso. They all stop at Osiadan.'

A brief silence ensued before the big chop-bar girl divulged that she still did not see the connection.

'I really don't see it quite clearly myself yet, either. But I've got a hunch that there is a connection.'

'So what should we do?' the girls wanted to know.

'I'll go and tell the police what I know. That way, I cover myself, and you too.'

◆

At the police station, when Mami Korkor arrived with her daughter, her son and his friend, had been introduced to Akua and heard all there was to know, she grumbled and snapped at her daughter, 'Why didn't an idea like this occur to me at your birth? It would have spared me the pain of having to live with your insolence now, or?'

And even though the police officer instantly reproached Mami Korkor for talking so cruelly to her daughter, Bibio herself didn't care a hoot. She treated her mother with such insolence that even the police officer winced.

But Mami Korkor ignored it and turned to the two boys. 'And you two,' pointing menacingly at them, 'now I hope you have grasped once and for all why I always tell you to stay clear of the rubbish dump. This time, thank God, it was just the clothing of a suspect. Next time, who knows? Go!' And she followed them out, still insulting them.

Akua watched their backs disappear and thought about the story of the man who felt he could not continue to live such a poor life and decided he would be better off dead. So he went under a tree, strung up a rope, removed his clothes, climbed on a chunk of wood and placed the noose around his neck, ready to die. Just then, an even poorer, more wretched man came by, saw the clothes under the tree, knelt and prayed, thanking God for coming to his aid with such good clothes, and took them. The man in the tree, realising that his situation was not the worst, removed the noose from around his neck, covered his nakedness with leaves and headed back home with renewed hope.

The police obtained a detailed description of Efia, and fed the information to the media. The following day, the papers carried her sketch – as well as the headlines calling for her blood.

Chapter 12

The knock sounded faint at first, then loud, louder and more urgent. Teacher stirred in her sleep, heard it again and woke up fully. She checked the time and growled. Who was this waking her up at 3:47 a.m.? She went to the door cautiously. 'Thieves?' she wondered, and shuddered.

'Who is it?' she hissed through the keyhole.

'Please, Teacher, it is me. Efia.'

'You?' And she swung the door open.

Efia stood there like a ghost in coloured clothing.

'What do you think you are doing here?' Teacher scolded and dragged her roughly inside. 'Do you know that they're looking for you everywhere?' When she closed the door, the stench of Efia's body hit her in the face, nearly knocking her off her feet.

'I've been hiding,' Efia explained morosely.

So Teacher made her take off her clothes, and heated water for her to take a bath. She then treated her to a warm cup of cocoa, which greatly helped to settle her.

Efia then told Teacher everything. The truth – starting from that day in Kataso when Teacher came asking her to be Tika's maid. And when she got to the issue of the birth of her daughter, she broke down in tears.

'So what happened?' Teacher prompted.

'The pains became severe, so I went and lay down in one of the rooms. It was unbearable. And then I realised the baby wanted to come. No one tells you that. God lets you know.' She paused again. Teacher did not interrupt.

'It was terrible,' Efia resumed slowly. 'Blood everywhere. Then it came out. And straight away I knew that something was wrong.'

'Why?'

'It wasn't right. It was like Maame Yefunbon's bad child. The evil child. The one that killed her. Remember?'

Teacher was aware of that Kataso woman's tragic story. She had had ten children, was warned against more births, ignored the warning, went in for an eleventh, and had a Down's syndrome baby. It was the first of its kind in Kataso, and the village was thrown into pandemonium. Accusing fingers were pointed, and three old ladies ended up being declared witches. They were driven out of Kataso. Libation was poured, rituals were performed and sacrifices were offered to the gods and ancestors to ensure that such an event never happened again in Kataso. And when Maame Yefunbon also died from excessive blood loss, her husband was made to slit the throat of a pure white fowl and drain the blood on to the feet of his wife's corpse to cleanse her soul before it reached the ancestral world. Since her death, no Down's syndrome baby had been born in Kataso again.

'So your baby was like Maame Yefunbon's evil baby?'

Efia nodded.

'And that was why you killed her?'

'No!' Efia was horrified. 'I didn't kill her. She died shortly after I bore her. She cried only once, very weakly. Then she didn't cry again, didn't move any part of her body, and stopped breathing.'

'So why didn't you wait to tell your friends and have her buried decently?'

'Because I thought that, because of all the bad things I and my people did, maybe Madam Tika had cursed us. Or that the gods and ancestors were showing their disapproval at what we had done. So I thought it was very important for me to return with the body to my people so that the necessary rituals could be performed to clear the curse.'

Teacher recollected that in Maame Yefunbon's case, the baby was sent into the bush for special rituals to be performed to see its soul off into the underworld, from where it was believed to have come, to prevent it from hovering over the earth and entering into another unborn child. She therefore understood why Efia felt such an urgent need to return to Kataso with the body.

'So I left the place where I'd been staying, packed my soiled clothes into a plastic bag and threw it on the rubbish dump. Then I left for the station and boarded a minibus for Osiadan. But the bus had a breakdown on the way, just before we reached Nkawkaw. The driver sent his mate to go and buy the part at Nkawkaw. By the time he came back and the mechanic had fixed the bus, it was much later. The sun was really hot. I had wrapped the baby in a small cloth and then put it inside a plastic bag and placed it in another plastic bag. But it began to smell so strong, not even the bags could hold it in. I had already aroused some suspicion because of the way I held on to the plastic bag. So when we got back on the bus and the smell got stronger, the passengers near me began to complain. When we reached Braha, a very quarrelsome woman, sitting right behind me, started shouting and grumbling. "We are dying in here," she screamed. "Driver, stop the car and let your mate check what is choking us."'

'And the driver stopped?' Teacher asked.

Efia nodded, lips pursed. 'They made us all get out. The driver's mate began to get out. Suddenly I felt the urge to urinate – I couldn't hold it in. Everyone saw it dripping down my legs. And embarrassing though it was, that was what saved me. I said I was going to ease myself and ran off. I removed the baby from the plastic bag and the cloth. I wanted to give her a decent burial. She was bloated and puffed, starting to disintegrate. I knew I couldn't carry her any further. So, the way things were, I decided the only thing I could do was to bury her decently, then return with my people to perform the necessary rituals. But then I heard noises, strange noises, which scared me. So I left her there in the thicket and ran off quickly. I got a lift to Accra in another car and hid in some bushes around Achimota.'

'Where you remained till now?'

Efia nodded.

Teacher digested what she had heard and explained to Efia that she had to give herself up. Efia agreed.

'And as soon as dawn breaks, I'll also go and see Tika, tell her everything and beg her to forgive you.'

Efia smiled sceptically, 'Would she?'

◆

Tika listened in stunned silence, a feeling of nausea in her entrails, bitter bile rising to her throat. 'They did all that in order to get their hands on my money?' she hollered, eyes ablaze with the fury of betrayal. 'And you thought you could just come and talk to me, beg me to forgive her and – oops! – all would be forgotten?'

Teacher kept her cool. 'I am as appalled by it all as you are, Tika,' she countered, 'but . . .'

'What?'

Which threw Teacher off balance, leaving her floundering for words. 'Maybe I hoped for too much,' she began at last. 'Maybe I shouldn't have come here to try to settle anything. But how could I avoid being drawn into this? It was me who found her for you after all, no? Though let's not forget, Tika, that it was you who asked me to find someone for you from your father's family. So I didn't force Efia down your throat. Still, like I said, maybe I hoped for too much.' And, abruptly and unceremoniously, she rose to leave.

That jolted Tika. 'Please don't go!' she begged ruefully.

But Teacher remained standing.

'Please, sit down!' Tika beseeched her.

Teacher acquiesced. And after a brief, highly charged silence, she said slowly and calmly, 'I came to suggest that we tell the police to let the matter of the family be handled by the family.'

Tika evidently didn't want to stretch matters too far. But she was also not yet in an absolutely conciliatory mood. So she asked coolly why she should agree to that.

'Nsorhwe, that's why!' Teacher stated bluntly, looking her straight in the face. 'You don't want to be blamed for the break-up of his family, do you? And his downfall too? Or?'

Tika considered Teacher's point, frowned, then said, 'Maybe all this is a web of deceit I also helped to spin. A web in which I too am entangled and from which I cannot simply extricate myself.' And with a dejected look she added, 'The money she stole – I never reported it, you know.'

Teacher heaved a sigh of relief. 'Thank you,' she said.

This was followed by a long silence which Tika broke, saying morosely, 'She was as much a victim of her people's manipulation as I was.'

'Yes,' Teacher agreed solemnly. 'She was.'

Tika pondered briefly, then asked, 'So did she really think that I had sent her to a juju man?'

'Yes,' Teacher replied, 'she did. Or that you yourself poured libation to the gods to invoke their curse upon her.'

Tika laughed bitterly and wondered aloud, 'So what do you

think would have happened had she delivered that damaged baby in Kataso?'

'I cannot even begin to think about it!' Teacher replied. 'But as sure as night turns to day and day to night, believe me, Kataso would have been thrown into a frenzied orgy of witch-hunting. And only God knows how many poor lonely old widows would have been spared. So we can thank God not only that Efia did not give birth in Kataso, but also that the remains were found in a state beyond identifying it as having Down's.'

'God help Ghana's poor, old, lonely women!' Tika muttered to herself.

'And God help us all!' Teacher added.

After another brief silence, Tika suddenly blurted out, 'I wonder though . . .' She broke off abruptly and paused.

'What?' Teacher asked, curious.

'Why do you suppose her highness, whoever she may be in the witches' kingdom, usually prefers poor lonely old women?'

'Could be a he ruling there too, you know,' Teacher quipped. 'In which case, the crucial question is why he would want to appoint wrinkled old women as his ambassadors on earth. He certainly seems to, if the rate at which such women are declared witches in our society is anything to go by.'

And now Teacher was wondering about something else. She decided to broach it and damn the consequences.

'Tika, about your mother,' she began, paused, saw that there was no reaction yet, and continued, 'She is not a woman of means any more, you know. She is growing old as well. And you, her only child, have also abandoned her. You know what that can lead to, or?'

Tika didn't need to be told any more to see what Teacher was implying, but before she could say anything, Teacher quickly set her a challenge, 'Why not go look for her?'

Tika thought for a moment and said contemplatively, 'Who says she would want to patch things up now? She was ready once, when I wasn't. Would she be now, just because I am?'

'Are you?' Teacher asked.

Tika shrugged, non-committal.

'If you are, then try!' Teacher urged.

But Tika's face stayed blank, betraying little of what was going on in her thoughts. Then, out of the blue, she asked, 'What do you think my father would want me to do?'

'Can't say,' Teacher replied carefully.

Tika laughed. 'Do you think he has been watching me all this time?' she asked Teacher.

'I have no doubt he has,' Teacher answered.

'Then surely you don't think that he approves of everything he's been seeing, or?'

'Like what?'

'Like the business discussions I used to hold in my bedroom!' And she burst out laughing and crying at the same time. Teacher joined in. And, together, they laughed and cried; laughing and crying away their pain, their disappointment, their anger, their fear. And laughing with hope.